How to Talk to Rockstars

How to Talk to Rockstars

by Alli Marshall

LOGOSOPHIA

HOW TO TALK TO ROCKSTARS
By ALLI MARSHALL

LOGOSOPHIA

Logosophia, LLC

Logosophia, LLC
90 Oteen Church Road
Asheville, NC 28805
www.logosophiabooks.com

This book is a work of fiction and thus of the author's imagination. None of the characters, places or incidents represented within have any real connection to any actual persons or places, living or dead, beyond the coincidental.

Library of Congress-in-Publication Data
Marshall, Alli
How to talk to rockstars
ISBN 978-0-9815757-8-0

Cover design and layout by Susan Yost
Cover art, "Glowingg" by Joshua Spiceland
Photography Carrie Eidson

For Tim, my favorite rockstar

Part one

At the edge of the stage, in the limbo between darkness and spotlights, between anonymity and fame, Jude Archer knows two things: That he is a rare genius. And that he is a complete fraud.

Sometimes he turns these dual realizations over and over like a penny in his fingers. Sometimes he lets them alternately punish and soothe his soul, these words. One a barb and one a balm. The devil and the angel on his shoulders, but which is which?

Sometimes he lets the needles of knowing fill him with doubt, with hope. With fear, with excitement. And sometimes he just turns away from the knowing, tucks the coin away into a pocket for later.

Or for never.

Just off stage, Jude Archer is no one. It's the moment of the day he hates most, those few seconds of not being. And then he hears his name.

For one night only—

And he's already in the light, bathed in it, blinded by it. Soaking it in and becoming. Not just someone, but the one.

All eyes are on him, and he's reflected back in their fevered glow. The one he's become. But which one? The genius or the fraud?

Fame, fame. Remember my name.

○

The terrible truth, thinks Bryn, *is that I can close my eyes and feel you in the air around me. Heat of your skin, scratch of your beard, even though I've never been in the same room as you.*

She blinks back into the present moment, pushes her glasses up on her forehead and massages her eyelids. For the hundred and tenth time she reminds herself that these details of Jude Archer that come so easily to mind are simply the work of an active imagination. Hers. He's no different from any other musician she's interviewed. She knows his bio and his latest album, *Fly By Night*. She knows a few details—his friends call him

Jim, he wears skull beads wrapped around his wrist, he has tattoos of his own design snaking up his arms and covering his chest.

Bryn does like to go into an interview with an arsenal of minutia. The tiny details make the person on the other end of the telephone seem more real, more whole. She needs a whole picture in order to move forward. In order to ask the questions.

Deep breath. Chase away the jitters, focus, find an inner calm. Then dial. The numbers click under her fingertips.

Sometimes the musicians call her. Or, if they're famous, their publicists call.

This is Amanda from Public Record. Hold while I get Marianne Faithful on the line. That sort of thing.

It's rare but not unheard of that Bryn calls in. Sometimes she's given the number and pass code to a conference call service where the voices of the different band members blur together until Bryn's ear learns who is who. What makes each voice unique.

But Jude Archer's number is just that. His number. She has it. Ever since it was sent to her, she's been careful not to look at it too closely. Sometimes the most benign things can burn. Now she opens the email, writes the number in black ink at the top of her notebook. Dials.

Not that anyone dials anymore. How long since she used a rotary phone, crossed time and space in the resounding clatter of the dial spinning back to zero?

Let it go. Focus.

The phone rings. Bryn breathes. Must be calm, otherwise there's a chance of squeaking out a greeting. She doesn't want to sound like a child. Relax, take time, speak slowly. This is Bryn Thompson with *Mic Stand Magazine.* Voice low and smooth, easy, warm.

He answers on the third ring, says, this is Jude. Sounds like he just woke up.

She says her name too quickly, adjusts her speed, asks if this is a convenient time for him to talk.

Yeah, it's fine.

Bryn cradles the receiver against her ear, watching the recorder measure the highs and lows of his voice. On the bottom end, the recorder barely registers. The skin on the back of her arms goose pimples. *How's your day so far?* she asks. *What city are you in this morning?* The throwaway questions. Usually she tries to breeze through those. Makes sure the

2

equipment is working and gets to the interview. Small talk only prolongs the awkwardness.

But his voice. Hoarse at the bottom and airy at the top. For just a minute she lets herself sink into it. Like when she was fifteen, stretching the phone cord to the basement stairs so she could talk in urgent whispers in the chilly dark.

Back when the dial clattered back to zero.

Bryn's coworkers are all at their desks, typing their own stories. She knows that they're at least halfway listening. She always halfway listens to their interviews. Knowing this is what pulls her back into the muscle memory of professionalism. The questions are in front of her on a scrap of paper, jotted down and scratched out, numbered in order of importance. She does what she's supposed to do.

Let's start with the name of the album, she says. And so it begins.

ii.

Bryn's first professional interview was not with a musician, but a ninety year-old art historian who had recovered work stolen by the Nazis. He was kind, but hearing-impaired, so she shouted her way through the interview. Because of a time zone difference, Bryn was in the office, alone, late in the evening. Sometimes loneliness bolsters confidence.

The basement staircase was that way. A dark stage to try on personas, words, ways of being.

There were failed attempts. Boys who, when Bryn dared to call, disguised their voices and said, no, he's not here.

Boys who said, uh, um, I don't know.

Boys who said, I don't really like you in that way. I don't *like you* like you.

✪

Sometimes it's that way with musicians. Bryn can hear their boredom and disinterest. It cracks like static from a cell phone racing across the desert in the back of a tour bus.

I don't like *you like you.*

Dig more deeply. Be more charming. Try a compliment, pull out the all-purpose questions:

- *Since you've been touring this album for [insert number of months], how has your relationship to this group of songs evolved?*
- *Any surprises?*
- *Any songs you especially love playing, or especially dislike playing?*

Sometimes something comes out of it. Sometimes the bored rockstar answers everything with Yes. No. I don't know.

✪

Jude Archer leans into the questions. That's a good sign. He says, good question, and pauses to think. Bryn feels her interior world expand into his pause.

He's not hers, of course. She has to share him with the world. With a world full of people who feel the way she feels. Like he speaks to them. Speaks for them. Puts into words the ideas and emotions they can't express. But he and she are similar in that way. Bryn doesn't have legions of fans who stand at the base of the stage and clutch their hands at their hearts while she plays, but she does work in words. She finds meaning in the ordinary, order in the drivel, golden in the mundane.

There must have been a moment when Bryn realized the weight—or was it the lightness?—of the written word. The *when* should be a tidy answer. The light bulb illuminating her path.

But no. Like most knowledge, it came in stages. The bitterness of spoken language and its fallible nature coupled with some early success on the page. A short story about a horse that was just a figment of imagination. A poem about a butterfly.

Bryn couldn't speak in class without stammering, she couldn't talk to boys without blushing, and when adults asked her what she wanted to be when she grew up, her mind went blank. But give her an essay question or a persuasive paper to write, and there was no limit to the words at her disposal. She wanted to live in the world of keystrokes and dictionaries, saying what she had to say on clean white sheets in neat rows of crisp black characters.

And then Bryn got older and the itchy little crushes on boys from elementary school—the ones that nagged at her but, if left alone, went away like unscratched mosquito bites—blossomed into the full-fledged rashes of high school crushes. She had to learn to reach past her shyness. It's probably love that brings any of us farthest in life. If not love exactly, than the heady potion of hormones that drives us toward sex by convincing us it's romantic love that we pursue.

It was a birthday party where Bryn sat under the stairs with a boy whose fin of blond hair fell over his dark eyes. They were both fifteen. They came there separately to hide from the others, to regain equilibrium in close space. They found each other and neither was surprised.

He peered at her with the same speechless despair that she so often felt, and so she wrote him a poem and tore the page from her journal. He read it over twice, folded it into a tight square and leaned in to kiss her. Lips like a soft bruise that would startle Bryn with an electric rush each time she remembered.

So then what? They are a pair of pale blond twins. He's taller, she's a few weeks older. When their lips touch, everything changes. Just a subtle shift, but still.

That was the second understanding of words.

✪

Tell me about the fourth wall in music, she says. *When you perform, is there an expectation of how your audience will respond?*

But of course there is. How could there not be? The musician goes into the studio to make his record. It's an artistic expression. And, as with any art, the creative process is only part of the finished product. The other part is the audience's response. But what artist creates without some expectation of that response? Would a writer finish a novel if she believed that no one would ever read it? Would a painter fill a canvas only to abandon it in a dark closet? Unlikely. Art is made to be experienced. And art is an extension of the artist. Art is made so that the audience can experience the artist.

The artist is the boy under the stairs with heavy-lidded eyes, willing his audience to kiss him.

Only it's not that simple, is it?

✪

The day that Bryn bought Jude Archer's album, *Fly By Night*, online and downloaded it to the playlist on her work computer—that was an ordinary day. It was three days before her birthday. She was working late. She'd just learned that she would have to work on her birthday, and the project was a dull grind. Her coffee had gone lukewarm in its tall ceramic mug.

The tracks appeared in order, summoned from some distant world. Bryn dropped the headset over her ears and clicked play. The world outside the headphones stood still. Blood beating in her ears, rivulets of rain streaking the picture window, outside a blurred watercolor. Everything and the absence of everything. A ballet of shapes and shapelessness.

Wanting seems so harmless at first, the way it feels like an old familiar ache, comfortable as pajamas. The way it feels good to return to a previous sadness, to sink into the soft gloom.

The way he spoke of love, always losing, always chasing, always wanting.

The songs held her captive from the first. She simply sat and watched the rain and listened. That was all. They were not acquaintances then, Bryn and Jude. They were two people in two separate bubbles. Bryn in her dusk-darkened office, Jude just a voice coming through the headphones. It didn't occur to her to wonder what he looked like, or his age or where he was from. Usually the back story was at the front of her mind. A journalist's habit. But Jude was a song first and a man later.

☯

It was Van Morrison, in college, who inspired in Bryn the art of deeper listening. *Veedon Fleece*, recorded decades before she would first hear it, caught her ear. Days stretched into weeks as she'd rush back from classes to sit on the floor in front of the stereo, spinning through the same ten songs. Every strange, unfathomable word stung at her soul.

Bryn was in love that fall. The kind of love that isn't love, just a juxtaposition of compulsion and imagination. But it felt so urgent, so necessary, that she willingly made a fool of herself over and over.

The boy, Tom, was retreating from the world and Bryn wanted to go with him. Bolstered by music and red wine, she'd visit him late at night and lay on his bed, talking to the ceiling about the images that the songs brought swirling to her mind.

☯

To write a good story, the writer has to care about the subject. Maybe not in a this-is-my-favorite-thing-ever way, but definitely in a this-particular-detail-intrigues-me way. The writer doesn't have to love country music in order to wonder why this particular musician wears a baseball cap instead of a cowboy hat, or why he uses his middle name instead of his last name, or what it's like to play the songs on a breakup-themed album night after night on tour.

Does it hurt, sharp and fresh, to step out on stage and relive the heartache? Or does the emotion somehow morph once it's been committed to lyrics and melody? Artists talk a lot about catharsis, and maybe there's something to it. Write it down and let it go. Or, maybe writing brilliant breakup-themed albums means constantly revisiting old wounds, scraping at the scabs until they bleed again.

The interviewer has to wonder.

- *What's it like to record, night after night, in an abandoned theater? Did you lose track of time? How did going days at a time without daylight affect your mental state?*
- *When did you transition from playing at being a musician to actually believing in yourself as a musician?*

The interviewer has to find the chink in the armor. Any musician who's been doing this for long enough—to take a serious tour, to hire a publicist and talk to more than a handful of journalists—has an arsenal of stock answers. It's hard for the journalist to break through, especially when the answers come easy and they're all the right answers. But right answers don't necessarily make for the right interview. The real interview. It takes a long time for the journalist to understand this.

Push through the stock answers. Find the broken places, the aches, the odd joys. Ask the questions whose answers don't make sense. Ask the questions that want to be asked. Listen for the answers that are begging to be spoken.

What did you give up to do this?
Who did you give up to do this?
How much longer can you keep going?
When will you know you've made it?

The answers—the *real* answers—come in the awkward pause after the stock answer has been recited. The writer has to learn to wait. Do whatever it takes. Breathe in, breathe out. Count to three or four or five. Resist the urge to be a sparkling conversationalist, to make the person on the other end feel comfortable by jumping in with happy chatter. Let the silence hang there, and the artist will fill it in. And that's when the real answer comes, on that unplanned and empty canvas.

❂

This can not end well.

And still. She lets herself go down the rabbit hole, that exquisite void surrounded by his voice and his music. A quiet video of him in the empty hallway of a hotel, sitting on the floor with his long legs stretched out in front of him as he plays a song. She wonders if he's as alone as he seems but no, of course not. That's the illusion. That's the thing that makes women fall in love with him. She must be smart and steel herself.

It was sometime between giving up on Tom and changing her major to journalism that Bryn stepped out of the train station and walked almost straight into a man. His long hair held back from his face by a ski cap, a couple days' growth of beard on his cheeks and a guitar case strapped over his back. She had seen at least a hundred guys in the same torn jeans and buffalo plaid shirt that week alone, but this one stuck with her. Brooding eyes. The way he really looked at her before moving away, down the stairs.

A couple weeks passed before she saw him again, and then it was in a bar where she'd gone to hear a new band that everyone was talking about. And he was fronting the band. That was Bryn's introduction to Preston Shotte.

The night was the brittle kind of cold where Bryn's breath crystallized in her lungs and getting inside, anywhere, was a relief. The bar was tight and steamy with bodies. It smelled of cheap beer and unwashed hair—the scent of Friday night anticipation hanging heavy in the air.

As soon as Preston stepped up to the mic, Bryn recognized him. She turned to her friend, said, I know that guy.

Her friend, the one who'd seen the band before and had obvious designs on its lead singer, said, really? *How?* Which was a fair enough question considering that, until that moment, Bryn had barely demonstrated an awareness of the male species as a whole, let alone a particularly stunning specimen.

Bryn had to let her mind roll through the index of meetings she'd had recently before hitting on the man outside of the train station, and she had to admit to herself that actually she hadn't *met* Preston Shotte, she'd only *seen* him. But strong eye contact surely counted for something so she said, we were on the train together.

Her friend probably would have challenged that claim, but the music came crashing out of the speakers and Bryn stuffed balled-up scraps of napkin into her ears making conversation doubly impossible.

Later, after the set was finished and the band had packed up, Bryn's friend went to work flirting and tossing her hair for the benefit of Preston Shotte while Bryn nursed a beer and felt embarrassed. She'd seen the whole ordeal plenty of times and it usually worked, which meant she'd be a fifth wheel on the way back to the dorms (unless Preston Shotte had a place of his own and asked the friend to go there). Usually she didn't care that much. It was vaguely entertaining. But this time, something troubled her.

Bryn kind of wanted to save him from her friend (though he was hardly a lamb among the wolves). And—not that she was willing to admit it in so many words—she kind of wanted to hang out with him on her own.

Eventually Bryn's friend went to the bathroom, leaving an empty barstool between Bryn and Preston. Hey, he said, noticing her for the first time. Bryn halfway wanted to sink into the floor, and halfway wanted to demand, *Don't you recognize me? Because we totally had a moment.*

Instead, she said, hey. Um, nice set.

Cool, thanks. He nodded, looked around.

Do you live here? she asked. In this neighborhood?

No, like ten blocks up.

Yeah, I saw you there, said Bryn. At the train.

Really, he said. So he didn't remember. It—the meaning of it—had been all in her head. But, even though she figured she should know better and she should quit before it got worse, Bryn couldn't just let it go. She could see her friend coming back from the bathroom, momentarily stuck in a conversation with someone but keeping an eye on Preston.

For my journalism class, we have to interview someone, Bryn said. It was a lie. She didn't even know where it had come from. But once she said it, the lie quickly grew: It's supposed to be published in the college journal. Anyway, I thought it might be cool to interview you. You know, about your band and all.

He looked interested. Wrote his number on a napkin and handed it to her. Said he didn't have to work on Wednesdays, if she had time then.

You two look friendly, said the friend, pushing in between Bryn and Preston.

Not really, said Bryn. We're talking about my journalism homework.

Homework. Boring, pouted the friend. Let's do shots.

But Bryn knew she'd won something. At least temporarily. Until she had to go through with the interview, which, she thought, maybe she wouldn't do. Wasn't it enough to have the rocker guy write his number on a napkin for her? Really, what more could she ask for?

There was more, though. In the next few days Bryn found that the more she tried to push the night at the bar out of her mind, the more she found herself thinking of things she wanted to ask Preston Shotte.

Where did you grow up? When did you know that you wanted to be a musician? Is guitar the first instrument you played? What bands did you like when you were in high school? What's the first concert you ever went to? When did you start to grow your hair? Do you hope to get famous?

11

Eventually she told herself she'd have to call. She'd call just once. If he was there and he answered, she'd set up the appointment and interview Preston Shotte. If not, she'd forget the whole thing.

When she dialed, her heart was in her throat. She found herself silently pleading with the universe for him not to answer, if only because she didn't think her voice would work. She'd squeak or croak. She'd die of embarrassment. It didn't matter. The questions didn't matter—

And then he answered the phone.

iii.

There's a moment, usually right before the person on the other end picks up the phone, when self-doubt descends like cloud cover and there's no way it's going to work. The questions are all wrong, the moment is all wrong, the room is too noisy, there's still more research to be done. Research to really understand a band, a sound, the nuances of the album.

There's a moment sometimes, not always, three or four questions in, when it's suddenly smooth and easy. Like talking to a friend. A favorite cousin at the family Christmas party. There's instant amicability, inside jokes, the buoyant feeling of like. As in, *he really likes me. This is cool. We'll meet at the show, we'll bond, we'll keep in touch. He might give me a shout out from the stage or maybe, someday down the line, include my name in the thank yous on an album.* Of course, all of that is ridiculous.

There's a moment just after the call is ended when euphoria kicks in. It's done, it was good. Interesting quotes were obtained but even better, there was a true sense of affinity. A connection. As in, *this is the best band ever and they're so under-appreciated. I'm going to write the story they deserve and get them their due recognition.* Also absurd, but well-intentioned.

There's a moment, at the beginning of writing, when the digital recording sits there on the computer screen, twenty minutes long and daunting. The mind goes blank—what was said? And how many minutes of hearing one's own voice must be endured? Because: *oh my god I sound like a complete moron. Biggest geek on the planet. I love your album—really?! That's original. And so sincere. Jesus, just stop talking already you stupid, over-caffeinated, chipmunk-sounding freak!*

There's a moment, somewhere around five minutes or seven minutes or maybe it's nine minutes, when the recording reveals that the rockstar on the other end is actually stuttering. Just a little bit. And it's kind of cute. Human, really. Deep breath, this isn't so bad after all. It's actually going well. And, *oh my god, he just laughed at my joke! A real laugh! I didn't even notice because I was too busy thinking about the next thing I was going to say. But I think he actually likes me.*

15

There's a moment when the story is almost done. Like, six hundred words in. And suddenly it comes together. It shines. It sings. It's really, really good, and with a little polishing, a few words changed, it'll be almost perfect.

Nothing's ever perfect.

But some things are close.

○

You can call me Preston, he said.

I thought I was.

Just Preston. You don't have to say Preston Shotte every time.

Oh, right, said Bryn.

They were sitting in a coffee shop where Bryn was drinking coffee and Preston was drinking a beer, even thought it was only just noon. Bryn scribbled on her notebook, testing her ballpoint pen for the zillionth time. I guess we should get started, she said. Suddenly it all seemed weird, and he was going to figure it out. That she'd contrived the interview just to be able to hang out with him.

Preston was wearing faded jeans and another flannel shirt. He'd hung a battered leather jacket over the back of his chair but left a striped ski cap on. His ponytail hung down his back in a tangle of walnut curls. The scruff of beard had grown into an actual beard, but despite his unkemptness, Preston was still attractive. Probably more attractive.

Bryn took a deep breath, and then a tentative leap: When did you first know you wanted to be a professional musician?

Oh man, since I was, like, fifteen, Preston said. He told a typical boy story about climbing out the window of his teenage bedroom and sneaking off with friends to see a band. How that night changed his life somehow. Bryn figured there was more to it, like *how* did that night change his life? Was it that *particular* band or could it have been any band? She wasn't sure how much to pry, so she moved on.

When did you get your first guitar?

When I was sixteen, said Preston. Actually, I was hoping to get a car, so when I got a guitar instead I was pretty pissed and I stuck it in the back of my closet. I was kind of over the music thing right then. I was into cars.

That time, Bryn pressed him: So what made you eventually learn to play?

He laughed, had a far-off look in his eyes. Broke my leg, he said. He

16

told a story about skateboarding. Something complicated that involved a contraband bottle of whiskey, a flight of stairs and a dare. In the end, Preston ended up spending summer vacation stuck in his room with a cast up to his thigh.

So you decided to teach yourself guitar? Bryn asked.

Not really, he said. I just ran out of comic books and I got sick of video games. I was looking in my closet for this porn magazine I thought I hid behind some stuff when I found the guitar.

Bryn felt herself turn red, but Preston didn't notice. He went on talking about how one of his buddies stopped by and taught him three chords, and then Preston started going through his record collection, trying to teach himself songs by ear.

A simple rhythm presented itself: Bryn asked questions (most of them obvious) and Preston rambled on while Bryn scribbled as much as she could into her notebook. An hour passed. If it had been a date, it would have been the easiest date ever.

Before they parted ways outside of the café, Preston said thanks and gave Bryn a hug. His leather jacket squeaked against her ear. He smelled of smoke and, more faintly, of dryer sheets. That realization—that Preston tumbled his clothes with Bounce—made Bryn's heart throb unexpectedly. Even after Preston's back disappeared into the crowd, and the day had passed and evening slipped into night, she still felt that strange ache. That burden of knowing something secret and intimate about another person; the way that knowledge makes the one who possesses it somehow responsible.

○

The thing that had to be done, of course, was to write the interview, and then to submit it to the school journal. Bryn did that; it was easier than she'd supposed. But life didn't change, except for a short-lived penchant for oversized flannel shirts and knit ski caps pulled down almost to the top of her glasses.

The clothes were a cocoon devised to keep Preston in (his hug, his clean laundry smell, his words) and keep out the harsh reality that he would never be hers.

Bryn did see Preston again. He started dating her friend, so bumping into him was almost routine. He said *nice story* in a way that made her think he hadn't done more than glance at it through a marijuana haze.

He said, hey, you don't know anyone interning at *Rolling Stone* this summer, do you? Because I wanted to get a demo to one of their reviewers.

You reference birds in almost every song on this album. Is there an ornithological interest, or are birds a symbol of something to you?

It's the fourth time Bryn has interviewed Evan Lassiter. She first met him when he was working in a record store full time and playing in three different bands in the evenings. Their first meeting is remembered only by Bryn. Evan didn't register her at all until a year later when she met him at a coffee shop overlooking the street where two gutter punks worked out an old time song on a battered guitar and fiddle.

Both, he says. Evan is alarmingly tall, but his voice is gentle.

I bought a house in the country, he says, and I've been watching birds a lot when I'm off the road. They serve as metaphors for a lot of things, you know? Freedom, but also loneliness.

It's interesting, right, how different birds stand for different things, Bryn says.

Doves for peace.
Cranes for long life.
Owls for wisdom or doom, depending on who you ask.
The phoenix for renewal.
Hawks for spiritual awareness.
Chickadees for optimism.
Hummingbirds for joy.
Swans for truth.
Crows are messengers or harbingers.
Storks are for good luck. Or for babies. Whatever.

Every meeting with Evan, other than that first one in the record store, has an album and a coffee shop associated. Bryn can recall them with the ease of flipping through a photo album. The self-titled debut: The Daily Grind—Bryn wore a purple t-shirt and her hair in a French braid.

The second album was *Caught in the green rushes with the tide going out.*

Dark Night of the Soul Coffee. Bryn wore denim trousers and red heels. Evan said, you look really well. Which was not the same as *you look really good*, and Bryn wondered about the difference for days.

The third album was *A Thousand Miles from Everywhere*. Evan was on tour with his band and they were all crowded around a narrow table at Iggy's when Bryn arrived. She was wearing a black jersey dress, one of her go-to outfits when she didn't want to betray anything with her clothes. The boys in the band were a jumble of black jeans, worn t-shirts and un-washed hair. Bryn felt her heart leap with both panic and familiarity. Evan rose to hug her. She put her arms around his waist and felt his hip bones through his clothes.

This album is *Early Frost*, its cover pearl gray. A row of pigeons on a telephone wire stretches across empty sky.

Bryn is in a striped grey shirt and a pair of skinny black jeans. Safe.

Evan looks even thinner, even taller. Gauntness suits him. His eyes are dark pools above his sharpened cheekbones. He's sipping pale, creamy coffee from a soup-bowl sized mug. They're at Black Magic, which is fre-quented by tourists and business people rather than the hipsters and artists they both know.

What did you give up to follow this dream? Bryn asks. As in, *what has music taken from you? What have you sacrificed at its altar?* She knows Evan was divorced, years ago. She knows he lived in a van for a while. He's been in at least a dozen bands, maybe a couple dozen. More than one band broke up over drugs. More than one former band member is dead.

His eyes are clear blue. Searching. He turns toward the window, rests his chin on his elbow. He crosses his long legs, says, nothing. I can't think of anything. This is the only thing I wanted.

He looks at her, and she recognizes the look. He trusts her. In the moment they're friends. She's familiar to him.

I was unemployed for a while, and not playing many shows, he says. I used to sit in my house all day and play music. I remember thinking that I could just keep doing that, just playing music by myself. Except eventually you run out of food and you have to make some money so you can eat. So if you want to keep eating, you've got to play for other people sometimes.

Bryn feels like she could stay there, listening. She wonders what else he'd trust her with. But she has what she needs, their time is up. There's no stopwatch, no sand dial. It's just a feeling. A sort of stop-while-you're-ahead feeling. She drains her coffee and stands up. Makes pleasantries. *It's always good to see you. Good to catch up. Hope to see you soon.*

By the way, Evan looks up from his mug. You're looking well, Bryn.

Thanks, she says.

✪

It's a nervous tick, smoothing her hair behind her ears. Bryn can't recall a time when she didn't do it. All through elementary school, middle school, high school and college she wore her long hair parted down the middle (sometimes with bangs, sometimes not). It always curled in a loose C shape toward her face on both sides as a result of being constantly wrapped behind her ears.

Once she started her first real writing job, Bryn cut her hair. First in a bob and later in a pixie. The short styles broke her of the habit of tucking her hair, and later, when she grew it back to shoulder-length, she could go days on end without a C curl.

But the tick came back, one of her tells, when she's anxious, worried or excited. There were other nervous habits, but Bryn taught herself to hide them.

Problem vs. solution
- Shakings hands: fold hands in lap.
- Looking like a dork: Carry a compact mirror and check teeth for food particles and eyes for smudged mascara.
- Feeling like a dork: Keep apparel simple. Black jeans, plain t-shirt under blazer or streamlined leather jacket. Black jersey dress with knee-high boots. No suiting, no khakis, nothing too trendy or tight or short.
- Being a dork: Be prepared. Have good questions. Don't joke too much, but be friendly. Don't talk too much, but be interested. And, again, be prepared. That cannot be over-emphasized.

✪

All summer, while the temperatures soar, hornets nest in the hollows of the steel guardrail that lines the pedestrian walkway on the bridge. Even at high traffic their metallic hum sounds a warning, like that of a live wire just waiting to strike, snakelike and vicious.

23

Now, on the last day of summer, heavy clouds bring early dusk and a fog of gnats swarms the neighborhoods. There's no way to dodge them, walking past dense boxwood hedges, but the hedges end before the bridge. The hornets have evacuated with the last of the swampy heat, and in the steel-blue dusk, it's a peaceful stretch of concrete and space.

On the other side, a man walks slowly in his cassock like the negative of a ghost. A squirrel darts and stops and darts again. Kitchens cast yellow light onto darkening lawns.

All of these images are fragments of songs that will never be sung. There is too much else between the pure thought and the execution, too many distractions, too many doubts. But the impulse is there. The seed.

We will someday run out of songs and we'll run out of coffee shops.

Or, *we'll never run out of songs and coffee shops.*

The actual truth is somewhere in between. Life has afforded us so many meetings. We don't know which number this one is. It doesn't feel like a final meeting, but it could be.

We are able to love best the things that are right in front of us.

Or, *we love best those things that have passed from us and can never be touched again.*

It's hard to know, in the moment. The first listen to a song is not necessarily the time when it infects the listener with its intoxicant. That could happen the third time, or the tenth. Or it might sleep within the psyche like a dormant virus, its true contagion not waking until a decade later. The song plays and the brain is flooded with images, sounds, smells, emotions from some time long past. And then it's too late. There is no antidote.

What we share is unique.

Or, *we are strangers who have become familiar through a job. But nothing else binds us.*

Or, *any bond is worth noting. Either through circumstance or coincidence we are connected in this world of randomization.*

On stage, Evan Lassiter genuflects his lanky frame over the body of his guitar. His hair is a curtain over his face, his eyes shutter out the audience. But his voice goes to all of the places his gaze won't dare. The corners, the rafters. He's singing the songs that Bryn has listened to a hundred times, the songs they spoke of, the songs whose secrets he revealed.

But he doesn't sing them for her. This she knows.

V.

There was someone once who sang to Bryn.

It was the summer after college, in the middle of August when the city seemed to empty out. Everyone who could afford to went on vacation. Bryn could barely afford ramen noodles, but she didn't care. The excitement of being at the beginning of everything was palpable, and a job as an editorial assistant at a small newspaper gave her just enough clout to be able to see bands for free. Not all bands, not stadium shows. But there was enough live music to keep her out late most nights.

One of those nights took Bryn into a bar that had little ambition beyond being a dive and yet, through some comedic twist of fate, ended up being popular.

She was sipping a cold beer, trying to fight off the heat of close quarters and sweaty bodies by holding the damp bottle against her neck, when she recognized the voice coming through the PA.

Preston.

Bryn made her way closer to the low stage, leaning against the wall to watch him. It had been awhile since she'd seen him—more than a year. She'd lost touch with the friend who'd started dating Preston after the college journal interview. And he'd changed in that time, she could see it.

After the set, Bryn stayed in her spot. She didn't move closer to the stage, but she didn't leave, either. She felt glued to that piece of wall, some passive-aggressive inner voice holding her there.

He won't even see you, said the voice. *And if he does, he won't remember you. And if he does remember you, he'll pretend he doesn't.*

Girls talked to Preston and flirted and eventually left, and then he unplugged his guitar and wound cords and began to carry his things to a car waiting outside. He passed by Bryn twice, the second time catching her eye. The third time he looked at her quizzically, trying to place her. Finally he came back and said, you interviewed me once.

She smiled despite her plan to play it cool. She said, I'm Bryn.

I'm Preston. He stuck out his hand.

27

I know, she said and placed her hand in his. He held on.

They made small talk. It felt easy.

Come with us, said Preston. My friend's waiting on me—we're going back to my place. You should come hang out.

She said okay.

They sat in Preston's living room, hours passing fluidly. They talked about nothing in particular. Movies, music.

Want to hear this new song I've been working on? Preston asked, his drunkenness not completely disguising his nervousness.

Bryn followed him to his room and perched on the edge of his bed while he sat in his desk chair and strummed the song.

It was a love song. A song about some other girl. But when he sang it, he looked at Bryn. He sang it to her. And when he rested the guitar against the desk, he leaned over Bryn and kissed her slowly.

Maybe she hadn't even known that's what she wanted.

No, of course she did. She wanted the song and the kiss and the boy. She wanted it all.

❂

There are a number of ways an interview can alter the like/dislike-to-band/musician ratio.

1. The writer likes the band/musician. The interview goes well. The writer either

    a. Continues to like the band/musician or

    b. Likes the band/musician more.

2. The writer doesn't like the band/musician. The interview goes poorly. The writer

    a. Continues to dislike the band/musician or

    b. Dislikes the band/musician even more.

3. The writer likes the band/musician. The interview goes poorly. The writer then can no longer continue to like the band/musician with the same enthusiasm.

4. The writer dislikes the band/musician. The interview goes well. The writer then

    a. Begins to temper her dislike with grudging admiration or

    b. Finds she can no longer dislike the band/musician in the manner to which she has become accustomed and

c. Eventually has to admit she likes the band/musician.

5. Wild card A: The writer hasn't formed an opinion of the band/musician. This is rare, but it happens. In that case, the turnout of the interview (good vs. bad) weighs heavily in the outcome of the writer's eventual like vs. dislike.

6. Wild card B: The writer has developed a level of like/dislike based on prior knowledge, research and the outcome of the interview. The writer then meets the band/musician and, based on that interaction, either

    a. likes them/him/her more or

    b. likes them/him/her less.

That's right. In the case of scenario 6, there is no chance of maintaining the same level of like or dislike. Meeting a musician in person changes everything.

✪

In the morning, Preston was a tangle of hair, one arm flung over Bryn's body, a leg kicked out in an attempt to reclaim the whole of his bed. He was sleeping deeply, snoring a little. Bryn propped herself up on an elbow and watched him for a minute, an inner monologue clanging in time to her headache.

He's just a boy. He's not that special, asleep. There's dried drool in the corner of his mouth. And he smells like beer and sweat. Beer sweat.

But he is special. He's lovely. He'll wake up and return to his former loveliness. He's the boy who sang to me, and that makes him beautiful.

She tried to fall back to sleep, but her head hurt too much. Finally she shook Preston until his eyes opened.

Huh?

I need aspirin, she said.

What?

For my head. I need aspirin, or whatever you have.

You're still here?

Yes—She wasn't sure how to take the question. Where else would she be?

It's in the bathroom, he said, and his eyes closed again.

Bryn padded to the bathroom. The floor felt gritty against her bare feet; the bathroom smelled weird. It didn't help that her head was throbbing. She found the aspirin in the medicine cabinet and stuck her head under the faucet to get a drink. She would have liked a shower, but there was no sign of a clean towel.

Back in the bedroom Preston was awake, but not out of bed.

Do you want to go for coffee or something? Bryn asked. Her stomach was tight with hunger.

I can't, I have a lot to do today. His voice was flat.

Where was the singing? Where did *that* guy go?

I could call you later, Bryn said. The moment the words left her mouth she wanted to stop then in midair. It was such a dumb girl thing to say.

I'll call you, said Preston.

It was a lie.

You have to go, said Preston. It's getting late and—

It's like eight a.m., said Bryn, but she was finding her sneakers, making sure her wallet and keys were in her purse. She wondered why she didn't notice the night before that Preston's apartment was so dirty, that he didn't even have a proper bed but just a mattress and box spring on the floor. Like a college dorm. Like the image that the words flop house called to mind. That Preston's hair was dried and split at the ends, that even though he was still in his mid-twenties it was receding at his temples and he was trying to hide that fact by pulling strands from the top down over the balding spot.

It's getting late and I have a lot to do, said Preston.

Which meant he had a girlfriend and she was coming over. They had plans. The sort of plans couples have. And it was probably the girl who had once been Bryn's friend, though Preston had not mentioned her name all night.

Bryn didn't ask. Nor did she say, *we didn't have sex. We fell asleep. You sang to me as I fell asleep. "Isn't She Lovely."*

She didn't say, *I hate you.*

She didn't say, *I don't want to hear your stupid album when it comes out. I don't want to see your stupid band ever again.*

She just walked out.

○

The terrible truth is that work is the antidote for loneliness. The preparation, the research, the obsessive listening to the album. Albums. As much of the back catalog as possible. It's all a key into the life of another person.

It's work, yes, but there are also moments when it feels cozy. Sometimes there's a blog, an online photo gallery, a tour journal. Of course, little of it is actually personal. It reads like confessions and insights, but to really understand the rockstar in question, it's a matter of deciphering clues.

There's honesty in the quiet spaces. In the moments when no one's looking. Candid photos. There's honesty, sometimes, in liner notes and in the lyrics of sad songs, but sometimes the truest moments come from happy lyrics.

There's honesty in silence, in what isn't said. In what's left unsaid. Seeking out these words and non-words means Bryn has to be a detective. Searching for clues, she's close to something. She's brushing up against another life.

And then the phone rings. There's a weird moment—*hi, how are you doing today? Are you in Santa Fe? How's your tour so far?*—where Bryn can't help but want to blurt something silly, friendly. She can't help but want to throw out a lifeline of friendship. After all, this is someone whose secrets she's riffled through as best as she could.

With knowing comes empathy. With empathy comes responsibility.

Bryn's mother asks, *why don't you go back to school and get a teaching degree? A nice college job would provide security. You could get tenure.*

She means, *writing about rockstars is not a real job.*

Bryn's mother asks, *at your age, should you be hanging out in bars talking to men?*

She means, *why don't you settle down with the sort of man you can bring home for Thanksgiving?*

Bryn's mother asks, *where is all this leading?*

She means, *where is all this leading?*

Bryn's mother asks, *are you happy? Are you eating? Are you using your vacation days?*

She means, *where is all this leading?*

Bryn's mother asks, *why not write for* ArtNews *or* The Atlantic Monthly? *They do such nice spreads.*

She means, *I can't read your articles myself, let alone show them to anyone.*

She means, *I tell my friends you write for* ArtNews.

Bryn's mother asks, *why don't you interview Mick Jagger?*

Actually, a lot of people have asked the same question.

But it's not about the questions that others ask. It's only the questions that Bryn asks. They can ask her anything. None of that finds its way into the story. What she writes, in the end, is what they say. That's the story. That's always the story.

❂

The terrible truth is that, for awhile, Bryn thought about getting into music reviewing just so that, whenever Preston Shotte's album was released, she could slam it. She'd tell the world what a jerk he was. She'd save other women from a similar fate. In fact, she'd deal with Preston and then she'd move on to the rest of the terrible musician-boyfriends out there.

It didn't happen that way.

She went back to school, worked on a Masters in writing, lived on black coffee and grilled cheese sandwiches. She thought for a while that maybe her mother was right. Maybe she'd write novels or screen plays. Something big.

But music called her back. It's what provided company while she studied, while she walked to class, while she sat in her apartment alone in the evenings and on the weekends.

Music was what she sought out. There were free concerts in the park and in the cathedral. She'd listen to a brass band rehearsing or to an Irish music jam. There were bars she knew from her newspaper job where she could go and nurse a single beer for hours while listening to a jazz combo or a singer-songwriter. It didn't matter what.

The thing was, to listen to music was to enter a conversation. It was to be in the company of thoughts and ideas that had been around far longer than Bryn had, and would long outlast her. Music was a language that required no translation. It was open to interpretation.

At some point in Bryn's life, she'd found Leonard Cohen. At some point she'd found Lynyrd Skynyrd. At some point she'd found The Righteous Brothers, The Doobie Brothers, The Avett Brothers, The Sabri Brothers, The Pointer Sisters, Sister Hazel, Scissor Sisters, Twisted Sister, Sisters of Mercy, Twin Sister and The Thompson Twins.

At some point she discovered KT Oslin, KT Tunstall, KD Lang, Jonny Lang and Lang Lang.

Zap Mama, The Mamas and the Papas. Papa Mali.

John Denver, John Mayer, John Lennon, John Lee Hooker, Johnny Winter, Johnny Cash, Johnny Rotten, John Mellencamp, John Scofield, John Phillips, John Coltrane, John Frusciante, John Legend, John Mayall, John Fogerty, John Zorn and Dr. John.

Sometimes she lay awake ticking off the names on her record collection, like counting sheep. Only obsessive and sleep-preventing.

Lyle Lovett. Ben Lovett. Lovett. Love. The Lovesix. Six Feet Under.

Bryn would listen to anything once. Gangster rap, Swedish death metal, post-disco, new age. It didn't matter. She liked what she liked, but everything else was still information. It was a language that she could tap. Can tap. Does tap.

And adds to. Sleepless nights are windows of opportunity for gathering new sounds, new words, new ideas. It's gotten easier over the years, even though people tell her that it's harder as one gets older to understand the music that young people like.

It's not like when we were young. Bands now are so [fill in the blank], they say. So loud. So caustic. So angry. So pointless. So electronic, no one even plays real instruments any more. So complicated. Why don't they just make music like they did back then?

Back when there was Pearl Jam. The Cure. Generation X. Television. The BeeGees. James Taylor. The Carpenters. Judy Collins. Bob Dylan. The Grateful Dead. The Beatles. The Monkeys. The Beach Boys. The Shirelles. Frank Sinatra.

Bryn thinks it's gotten easier. If someone wants to understand, all the information is right there. When she was a kid and heard a song on the radio, she'd have to sit there, glued to the station, just hoping the DJ would announce the song title and who sung it.

It could take weeks of waiting. That's how she got "Slip Sliding Away." That's how she got "I Ain't Missing You."

First there were records and later, tapes. Bryn loved tapes. All through high school she kept them in shoeboxes, organized under her bed. She had a dual tape player in her bedroom and she'd painstaking compile mix tapes, gluing images torn from magazines into thoughtful collages for the covers. These, of course, were given as shy gifts to boys.

Boys who dumbly refused to understand the thinly disguised messages in The Police's "Every Breath You Take," Elvis Costello's "Mystery Dance," Suicide Twins' "Heaven Made You."

CDs came next, but without the romance of records. Bryn harbored secret crushes on the college boys who DJ-ed raves, storing vinyl records in plastic milk crates. The heft of those crates, the library-like reference base of material—it meant something. CDs in their easily-broken jewel cases were only temporary.

Bryn was only too glad to sell off most of her CDs as soon as she was able to build an MP3 library. The iPod replaced the Walkman. She could organize playlists on her phone. Playlists for work and home. Music stored on remote internet databases to be accessed from anywhere. Everywhere.

To never be cut off from music was the answer to some question surely uttered decades, even generations ago.

To never again hear a new song and have to go on, not knowing what it was—that was technology at its best.

John Waite. Aaron Waite. Tom Waits. Tom Petty. Tom Tom Club. Rob Thomas. Chris Rob. Chris Robinson. Mark Robinson. Marky Mark. Michael Mark. James Mark. Money Mark. Eddie Money.

Eddie Vedder.
Eddie From Ohio.
Finish the chain, she'd think. *What's next? Ohio what? What?*

vii.

He was from Ohio. Jude Archer from Ohio. It would have been a terrible band name, but it was one of the first facts Bryn found in her research. Whenever she was interested in a band, she'd look up the musician's hometown and his or her birth date. Age and zodiac sign. It was a guilty pleasure, a habit she never admitted to anyone.

But it also revealed a lot. A thirty-nine-year-old Libra from the Midwest was a completely different animal from a twenty-seven year-old Pisces from Los Angeles. Bryn planned her questions accordingly.

- *This is heavy subject matter. How hard was it, emotionally, to write?*
- *Do you find inspiration in travel for new material?*
- *This album has a sense of immediacy. How were you able to create that in the studio?*
- *You say it was always your dream to be in a touring band. Now that you're on the road full-time, what parts of it are not living up to your expectations?*
- *When you come home now, are you able to get right back into the routine of being at home, or do you feel lost and disoriented?*
- *Are you who you thought you would be?*
- *Are you where you wanted to get to?*
- *How will you know when you've arrived?*

Bryn thinks of these questions as she listens to Jude Archer's album. Of course, this is backwards. To listen to the most recent album first, and then work back toward the debut—especially when the musician has an extensive catalog—is to see the reveal before knowing what the magic trick is.

It's to know the outcome without the benefit of the lead up. The failures, the heartache, the tears. The bruises and scrapes. The moments of despair. It's the perfect vision of hindsight.

Perhaps that's how the musician would want it. To seem to have arrived here, at this point, whole and self-assured. Forget the embarrassing sophomore album, forget the experiments with drum machines, the foray into folk, the haze of drugs, the breakup songs, the wincingly bad haircut, the white leather pants.

It's Bryn's job not to forget. Even more so, it's her job to find out. To crack songs like safes leading to raw nerves and diary entries.

To know and to ask.

Or, sometimes more importantly, to know and to not ask.

He answers on the third ring, says, this is Jude. He sounds like he woke up recently.

She says her name too quickly, adjusts her speed, asks if this is a convenient time for him to talk.

Yes, it's fine. His voice is hoarse at the bottom and airy at the top. For just a minute she lets herself sink into it, but she doesn't submerge. She's in it and of it, but she's also above it, seeing everything. She eases her mind, closes her eyes for just a moment. Allows herself to see him as she's imagined him, the him of details and facts. The boy from Ohio, the boy who's mother must have worried through lost weeks until he resurfaced in a dingy apartment or maybe a hospital. The boy who woke up one day and was a man with a dim memory and notebooks full of scrawled poems.

Heartache, angry rash, longing for something unnamable, unfathomably blue sky through the one smudged square of window.

The questions are in front of Bryn on a scrap of paper, jotted down and scratched out, numbered in order of importance. She does what she's supposed to do, what she knows best.

Let's start with the name of the album, she says. We'll start there and see where we end up.

Part two

The time between beginning to research an artist and doing an interview was usually just a couple of weeks. Sometimes a month, but that was rare. The magazine printed monthly, and the online edition came out every week. Bryn stayed busy.

With Jude Archer, though, it was different. He wasn't an assignment. Bryn discovered his album one day while procrastinating. Well, not really *procrastinating*. It was part of her job to listen to new music, to know what was out there.

She downloaded *Fly By Night* onto her iPod and listened to it on the way home from work. Then she listened to it on the way back to work. She listened to it while eating her lunch. She listened to it while going for a run, while shopping for groceries, while fixing her hair, while cooking dinner.

It was two weeks in, after idly Googling Jude Archer at least a dozen times, that the plan began to form.

Interview him.

No. Bad idea.

Only, why not? Interviewing rockstars was her job. He was a rockstar. He had a new record—a really *good* record. People needed to know about it. She could tell them. She could help Jude Archer tell them.

Bryn let another week pass, and then, when the songs continued to play automatically in her head, she looked up Jude Archer's publicist.

○

Bryn's first in-person interview of her career (not counting Preston Schotte) was, thankfully, with a woman. Chelsea Blake. Not that being female made her any less intimidating. She showed up twenty minutes late to the coffee shop she'd picked, her shaggy black hair falling over her large black sunglasses. She dropped heavily into an armchair, pulling the glasses off and revealing raccoon rings of eyeliner.

Chelsea Blake looked good, though. Even with bed head and slept-in makeup. Even in a worn black trench coat, a crumpled man's dress shirt and black leggings tucked into high-heeled boots.

Jesus, I'm hung over, she said by way of a greeting.

Bryn won points by ordering Chelsea a tall black coffee with two shots of espresso and a ton of sugar. You want something to eat? Bryn offered. Bear claw?

Bear claw, Chelsea snorted at the pastry. Everyone's favorite from childhood. Then: Yeah.

In between gulps and bites, Chelsea told the meandering tale of her previous night's exploits. She pretty much ignored Bryn's questions. She rambled, she embellished. She talked, for the most part, like the guy musicians Bryn had interviewed—only more so. Chelsea Blake, Bryn realized, was a woman in a man's world, and she was willing to compete on men's terms. She rocked hard, she partied hard, she occasionally went home with a fan or a guy from the band she'd opened for, or a guy from the band that had opened for her. She was known for sleeping with the guys in her band, and then acting like a complete maniac and driving the guy out. Chelsea Blake had gone through five bass players and three drummers. Her only consistent member was her guitarist, who was also her brother.

One of the main rules for interviews: Control the conversation. Do not let the subject run off on a tangent, go off topic or miss the question all together.

Another rule: Sometimes the rules have to be abandoned.

Chelsea Blake was the exception to the rule. That was probably the story of her life, and Bryn found herself wanting to tell *that* story. So she gave up on her questions—

• *In what ways have you had to confront sexism as a female band leader in the very male world of rock music?*

• *Do you remember the moment you knew you wanted to have a band?*

• *Whose career would you most like to emulate?*

• *How much of a factor is fashion in your stage presence and live performance?*

—and instead folded the piece of scrap paper, on which her questions were written, and tucked it into her pocket. She said, making sure the tape recorder registered her voice, do you mind if I use what you're telling me in the article?

Huh?

The story. About last night. Is that on the record?

Oh, yeah, sure, Chelsea said. She took a lipstick from her purse and applied it, using her coffee spoon as a mirror. She said, whatever, man.

Truth: There was something ridiculous about Chelsea Blake. She lacked the filters that would have prevented her from saying, *this dude was dumb as stump, but hot, you know? And it's not like I was ever going to see him again, right?* But there was also something fascinating. Something fabulous. Her dirty but gorgeous face. Her ruined but cool clothes. Her slouch, her pout, the way she smelled of perfume and cigarettes.

Bryn found herself both repelled and jealous. Wanting to tell Chelsea to stop saying those crazy things. To pull it together, fix her eye makeup. But she also wanted to hang out with Chelsea, maybe borrow a t-shirt or a pair of heels. Ask her for hair advice. Look at her photo albums, maybe see what she carried in her purse.

Like/dislike. A powerful combination.

○

A chilling draft. A fever. A headache deep behind the eyes that won't cease, won't be relieved. Bryn huddles under the duvet and allows her mind to wander. If a fairy godmother appeared right at that moment and offered her a deal: trade her career and whatever ground she thought she'd gained for one kind-hearted person to sit with her through the virus, Bryn would take it.

A cool hand against a burning forehead. A soothing voice. Someone to bring cold water and hot soup. Someone to offer a back rub, someone to draw a bath, someone to sit there and talk. Just talk. About anything.

It was rare that anyone would ask about her. Why would they? It was her job to ask. It was their job to answer.

(*Remember: You're not friends. Not friends.*)

The Irish singer wanted to know, what do you most like about being a music writer? Because before I had this band, I was a writer, too, he said.

Bryn said, so when you're doing interviews, do you find yourself wishing you could tell the interviewer what to ask?

But he was too good-natured and too professional for that. He said that having been there made him appreciate the person on the other end of the line. That he was glad for anyone who took an interest in his band and helped spread the word.

At the time, American Celtic-rock bands were surging in popularity.

The Dublin lilt had worn off the edges of the Irish singer's accent from years lived in Los Angeles.

If you were the interviewer, what would you ask me? Bryn said.

He laughed, asked her if she had a secret novel-in-the-works printed out on the office printer and hidden in a desk drawer.

No, not me, she said. But it was a good observation about writers in general. The clichéd dream.

Rockstardom—especially rising rockstardom—came with its own set of clichéd dreams. The big two were:

1. To make enough money to be able to get a bus and go on tour
   a. Across the U.S.
   b. Across Europe
   c. Across Japan
   d. Across Australia
   e. Etc.
2. To make enough money to park the bus and tour less and
   a. Just work on albums
   b. Just play the really prime venues and festivals
   c. Buy a house
   d. Start a family
   e. Have some semblance of a normal life
   f. Etc.

After that, the dreams were about opening for so-and-so, co-billing with so-and-so, collaborating with so-and-so, having a gold album and making lots of money. People wanted to be famous, though very few people claimed to want the sort of fame that came after death. Not Nick Drake fame. Not the sort of fame that comes from doing good and meaningful work in life that goes widely unrecognized and then, years and years later, is suddenly appreciated.

Rockstardom does not worry about the long term. It's about the moment, the now. No one worried that his or her sound would be stale or passé in two years. No one worried that he or she would actually achieve some level of prominence only to be washed up and laughed at a few years later. The punch line to a joke. The Milli Vanilli, the MC Hammer.

Bryn knows the statistics, at least in general terms. Of those who set out to make it in music, only a few will succeed. And success is hard to define. There are so many milestones—making a record, going on tour, getting a label deal, getting a tour bus, leaving the U.S., having a hit single, getting a magazine cover, selling a song to a movie sound track or a commercial. Making enough money to live on—that's one of the hardest marks to hit, and the most important. But few people mention it. Solvency smacks of reality, and little of the rockstar dream has to do with reality.

Reality is for the people who stay home, stay employed and buy tickets to the shows so they can taste the dream without ever having to risk all of the uncertainty.

Dreams are for people who live on hope and adrenaline. Champagne, romance, Cimmerian nights and regret.

But dreams also have a way of keeping dreamers warm against the cold drafts of the real world. Responsibility, monotony, loss, sadness, illness, poverty (or joyless wealth), disillusionment. All of these things were part of real life, but dream life offered the promise of something better. Something brighter, shinier, more exciting, more glamorous, more fun.

This is what Bryn thinks about, in and out of fever, as the shadows move across the room. And then she falls into dreamless sleep, and then she wakes and considers her shelves of CDs and records. Eventually she wraps herself in a thick bathrobe and shuffles across the apartment to her bookcase where she finds a novel that she's been meaning to read but never quite has the time for.

The room is silent. It cools and darkens in silence. Below, on the street, people call and traffic moves to its own rhythm. An occasional siren, a dog, a child, the clank of machinery, a distant train. But in the room, the air is still. A lamp casts away the gloom of evening. Unspoken words replace music.

○

The editor wanted to know who'd take the Dex Dansen story.

Pisces. Born in 1967.

His publicist says he's being a bit, um, difficult, said the editor. No one else in the office was making much eye contact. They were busy checking email, picking hangnails, examining the stained carpet with great interest.

I'll take it, said Bryn.

She wanted to listen to *The Bored and the Beautiful*. She wanted to be in his world.

What's it like to be beautiful, and how do you feel about time robbing you of that beauty?

47

Do you care what people think of you? Do you listen to what they say?

He'd tell her, I just want to talk about the album.

But she did wonder about the rockstars who were more image than sound. The ones who couldn't seem to get out of their own way to make their message heard. Was there even a message? Or just hollow beauty?

Hallow beauty.

Bryn had to admit to herself that she liked to be close to the beauty. The flame. The cool-burning heat of fame (or near-fame), the insouciance of it. The unpredictability.

It didn't matter if Dex Dansen didn't like her. Just to hang out in his gravitational pull for a little while would be worth the self-doubt, the cold sweat, the throat-tightening awkward moments. (Hers, not his. Obviously.)

She walked down the hall to the bathroom and stood in front of the mirror, assessing herself. She was dressed in the uniform that she'd developed over the years. Black jeans, a striped t-shirt and ankle boots. Understated and appropriate for most occasions. She never felt particularly fashionable, but she also almost never felt wrong. For a nice dinner she'd throw on a blazer and some eyeliner. Probably ninety percent of the time she felt fine. Six percent of the time she was sick or had cramps or whatever. The other four percent (note: all of those percentages could be interchanged) was lingering insecurity and *Oh my god I'm going to interview Dex Freaking Dansen.*

It was hard not to tell everyone. Her mom. Strangers in the grocery store. The plumber.

The weird thing, of course, was that when people did know, they always said the same thing: Oh, cool.

That's it. As if she'd said, I saw Dex Dansen in line at the post office.

Oh, cool.

I got Dex Dansen's signature at a concert.

Oh, cool.

I'm going to Tuscany for the summer with Dex Dansen. You know, of The Bitter Pills? Because we're tight like that.

Cool.

After awhile, she stopped talking about it. Besides, talking to the rockstar was, ultimately, such a small part of the equation. Most of the story was just her, alone with her research and the albums, a ream of back interviews and her own perceptions.

It was about her relationship with the artist.

In the end, the interview time came and went, and Bryn sat alone by her silent phone. An hour passed, though she knew by fifteen minutes in. He wouldn't call. Eventually the publicist called, said Dex Dansen wasn't available after all. He couldn't do the interview, and he wouldn't be able to do it later, either.

Bryn sat for awhile longer with her notes in front of her. She read over them again and scratched out a couple of unfortunate word choices. She felt sort of like a blind date left sitting in a restaurant, picking her way through the bread basket and watching the ice melt in her water glass.

The blind date knew, almost immediately, that she was being stood up. There's a sense. The first five minutes, she chides herself for being cynical. Ten minutes in she takes a different tact. *I hope he isn't hurt. I hope nothing bad happened.* At fifteen minutes, she gets angry. *When he shows up, I'll let him know he should have called. Being late is one thing but not to call?* And finally, at twenty minutes, she begins to accept what's happening. It's just a matter of how much longer she needs to sit so that, when she leaves, she'll know she was, indeed, stood up. She won't be left wondering if she'd just given it ten more minutes...

But no.

And then all the lead up, all the one-sided conversations, all the what-ifs, all the projections of happily-ever-afters—all of that has to be unraveled.

There was never to be a happily-ever-after with Dex Dansen. All he denied Bryn was an interview. A story that she alone would get, and then not get. But he also denied the place she'd set for him at the table.

It happened, though. Rockstars, by nature, were required to turn down a certain number of interviews. And reviewers, by nature, were required to not really care. So Bryn learned to play her role, keeping a backup plan at the ready, trying to find the balance between not doing enough research and over-investing herself.

She learned to draw a line between respect and admiration, and actual love.

Love was for real people. Flesh-and-blood people. People who called. People who showed up for coffee and for movie dates. People who were there after work and on the weekends. People who were not rockstars.

ii.

- *You went from being a rock band to more of a California country band. How did that happen?*
- *How much is your sound influenced by living in Laurel Canyon, and is that place infused with the energy of its previous famous residents?*
- *It's only been two years since you released your debut album, and you're already playing stadiums. Does it feel like everything has been moving really fast?*

There comes a day when the musicians on the other end of the phone (and across the café table and on the stage) are suddenly, and without warning, younger than Bryn. First, they're three and five years younger, which is nothing. Then they're ten years younger, which is alarming. Then they're fifteen years younger, which is just laughable.

They're not getting older. As a whole, the rockstar race remains steadfastly anchored between the ages of twenty-one and twenty-seven.

Writers, apparently, don't have a pipeline to the fountain of youth. The young ones are thirty far too early, the rest are preternaturally middle aged and get older from there.

I'm so nervous, says the guy on the other side of the office. This is the guy who never lets anything bother him. The guy who crashes on friends' couches instead of wasting perfectly good beer-drinking and festival-going money on rent. The guy who lives in the same jeans and flannel shirt and somehow never looks anything but artfully disheveled. But he's waiting for Wayne Coyne—or rather Wayne Coyne's publicist—to call. It's eleven minutes, and then seventeen minutes and then twenty-three minutes past the assigned time of the interview.

I just want it to happen, or know it's not going to happen so I can stop feeling like this, says the guy.

Limbo is more hellish than hell.

The guys who become music writers are often, though not always, failed musicians. Not even failed, really. Would-be musicians who didn't have real talent, or the patience to learn, or the stomach for show business and weeks on end trapped in a cramped van, living off fast food and diesel fumes.

The guys who become music writers are often cool, but with a nerdy proclivity toward music snobbery. They have their pet bands, their vinyl collections, their vintage concert t-shirts gone sheer with wear. They can recite facts. They'll argue passionately about why Wilco is better than Sun Volt (or vice versa). They are the instant buddies of the bands they interview.

The girls who become music writers are few and far between. Most are in their twenties. Just out of school, dressed in denim, wearing their hair long and pulled into a messy pontytail, the whole look augmented with black plastic-framed glasses. Girl music writers tend to be a disorienting mix of sexy and smart. If they stay with it, they tend to adopt an armor of toughness, armed with facts and opinions, not afraid to ask hard questions.

Writers eventually grow up and become editors. Managing editors. Publishers. Only musicians remain, forever, in their timeless limbo.

Limbo, for those who can hack it, has its benefits. Its lack of responsibilities, its freedom from business dinners, conferences, meet-and-greets, My Name Is tags.

What makes the story really interesting, though, is when both the writer and the artist have grown. Are growing. Are stretching beyond the constrictions of those first thrilling months and years in the skins of their respective careers.

- *By changing the name of the band, you took a big risk. But were you also able to shed some baggage?*
- *How much thought do you put into the order of the tracks?*
- *People have been calling this a concept album, but, ultimately, aren't all albums concept albums?*

The guy across the office takes a sip of water. A deep breath. Stands up and adjusts his denim jacket, rakes a hand through his hair, walks to the window and gazes out over the street like he has all the time in the world. As if by playing nonchalant, he'll trick himself into feeling that way.

Bryn feels sorry for him, but she keeps her eyes on her own computer screen, smoothes a lock of hair behind an ear. It's a courtesy—pretend not to hear another writer's interview, pretend not to notice his stumbles and stutters, pretend not to pick up on the fight-or-flight dance of nerves and excitement.

She's been there. Sometimes it's not as bad. Sometimes it's worse. It never goes away.

The guy takes a deep breath, bounces up and down on his toes like he's readying himself for a race.

The room is deep in shadow but outside, the day is bright and warm. A street musician sings a few bars of a song by Tonic and the office groans collectively. Time moves, sluggish but determined.

On the desk, the phone rings. The guy reaches for it, already beyond the panic. Already on autopilot.

○

Robert Lamar plays a small show in a dimly-lit listening room. Bryn goes, despite her trepidation. His broody songs and frightening (e.g.: homeless) look have always kept her away from his shows in the past. But lately she's been in a mood to see everything. She doesn't want to stay in. Being out, just about anywhere, is better than being in.

So, she goes to the show and sits at the bar, sipping a beer, watching the crowd as much as the show. More men than women. Lots of couples. More people are over forty than under forty. Everyone is paying attention, though the singer never once makes eye contact with the audience. He closes his eyes when he starts the song, and when he's not singing, he shuffles toward the back of the stage like he's lost.

What makes people love music? Why one band over another? And why do some people love one band that others can't stand? Why are music fans willing to pledge loyalty to a band, a musician, a record or a song? Because music isn't tangible—not exactly. A song is not a commodity. It can be shared but not saved or spent. It doesn't increase in value, and if it decreases that's only because the laws of what's cool, what's *in* and what's of-the-moment are fickle.

So. Why Jude Archer and not Robert Lamar?

It sounds like the Rolling Stones or Beatles question. It's not. But Bryn has known the answer to that one for a long time: The Stones. That the world could potentially be divided into Beatles fans and Stones fans is slightly disturbing to her. How different are the two bands, anyway? They started at roughly the same time. Both white, both British, both had shaggy haircuts.

Both have had way too much radio play.

53

That their two sounds could spark an ideological rift is just weird.

An hour into the show, Robert Lamar sets down his guitar, jumps off the front of the stage and walks straight out of the club, hops into his truck which is parked by the door, revs the engine and drives off.

Everyone, including the sideman, is mystified. The house lights come up and recorded music fills the speakers. People remain in their seats for another minute. They've been trained to clap and cheer and demand an encore. It's tradition. This predicament makes no sense.

From her perch at the bar, Bryn watches the confused fans come to terms. They've seen it before. Welcome to the Robert Lamar experience, someone says. The people around him laugh warmly, happy to be in on the joke.

Beatles or Stones?

Mariah or Celine?

Loretta or Dolly?

Kenny or Willie?

Bob Dylan or Joan Baez?

No, that last one can't be an either/or. There would never have been a Bob Dylan without a Joan Baez, even if they were never a couple, even if their time spent together was a mere minute on the clock face of eternity.

iii.

*   *Were you afraid of the sophomore curse?*
*   *Does it feel like a milestone to have the third album completed?*
*   *Do you ever revisit the songs from your first record, and, if so, how do they make you feel?*

Bryn ticks off the questions as she asks them. She's listening to the person on the other end of the phone, but also idly checking her email, opening an envelope, Googling band photos online.

The sophomore slump: A real or imagined curse in the music world. Make a good first album and everyone is waiting for you to fail on your second. The second album plays out like this:

1. If you don't fail, they say it's because you played it safe and made the first album all over again.

2. If you try something different, people say you're inconsistent and that you're alienating your fan base.

3. If you take a risk and it fails, they say you don't have what it takes to sustain a career.

4. But if you take a risk and it pays off…well, then you've got a target on your back for that third album.

   a. But people also grudgingly respect you.

   b. And your fans think you have super-powers.

Bryn had a sophomore slump once. It lasted through most of her twenties. It lasted as her friends paired off, moved in with significant others, married, moved up in their careers and put down-payments on apartments in semi-enviable neighborhoods.

Bryn went to shows, spoke to strangers and dated (sporadically) an experimental jazz guitarist named Spike (probably not according to his mother) who was signed to an obscure-but-important label and spent most of his time touring Europe.

You could come with me, he said.

But Bryn really couldn't. She didn't earn much at her newspaper job, and she had rent and student loans to pay. A month spent riding trains around Europe was only slightly closer to reality than winning a Pulitzer for her in-depth interview with Sean Lennon.

The guitarist, Spike, spoke about music in terms of 'post' and 'meta' genre classifications. Nothing was what it was, everything was what it once had been or might some day become.

Spike cut his hair in an ironic faux-hawk and then an ironic mullet. He grew an ironic beard. When he played grungy punk clubs he wore a suit; when he played nice concert halls he wore a vintage Armani jacket with a Batman t-shirt and Converse low-tops. He wanted to live in the Bronx or in east L.A., some place that was post or meta. Some place that had been or might be, but wasn't at the moment.

Of course, he believed that by being there, *him* being there, the place would be able to rise to its potential.

Bryn liked Spike and his misguided sense of importance. She liked to listen to him talk about music, even though he was pretentious and a bit of a bore. A bore, but never boring. Spike unwittingly taught her the difference.

He was in Europe when his latest album came across her desk. She'd worked her way up to an assistant arts-writer position at a weekly.

The job also entailed maintaining the entertainment calendar, a tedious and time-consuming task that left only a few hours each week for reviewing albums or shows. It was almost a pleasure to say to her editor, I can't take this one. I'm dating the musician.

The editor picked up the CD and studied it. Spike Robins? Really? You're dating him?

Bryn nodded, nonchalant. She tucked her hair behind her ear. In regard to Spike she had always done her best to downplay it. And he had often said as much. *You're so chill. Not like other girls. Never saying we should move in, we should get a puppy, we should spend more time together.*

The editor said, it's just that I thought he was dating that Swedish singer, what's her name?

He had already set the CD back down and returned to whatever he'd been working on.

The story, in its retelling, took on the tarnish of a bad soap opera. Bryn quickly quit telling it. The breakup lacked drama—Spike was gone all the time, anyway, and after Bryn got his side of the story *(She's my* Europe *girlfriend, Bryn. I have two lives. You can understand that, right?)* he just didn't come back.

It was simple. It was mutual. It was clean.

Were you afraid of the sophomore curse?

Not the freshman fifteen. Not senioritis.

Bryn wasn't afraid of the sophomore curse, because she never saw it coming. If she was afraid of anything, she was afraid, once she was in it, that she wouldn't find her way back out.

She was in the maze, deep in the labyrinth. At first it was an adventure. A dark and rather unpleasant adventure, but an adventure nonetheless. After awhile, though, the maze was all there was. Each turn led to a dead end, each twist spun her dizzily on her axis, leaving her increasingly uncertain of where she'd started, which way she'd come from.

The maze was all there was. Bryn began to wonder if that's the only place she'd ever been.

Spike had looked like a way out. Turned out, he was another dead end. The labyrinth prevailed and the sophomore curse wore on.

You should get back out there, Bryn's friends said. *Meet another guy.*

So Bryn got back out there. But not to meet a guy. To meet the one date who had never failed her. Music.

❂

Jazz bands, rock bands, country-blues. Bluegrass, torch songs, doo-wop, be-bop. Hip-hop, spoken word, pop. Indie-pop, indie-rock, alt-rock, post-alt-rock. Metal. Soul, neo-soul. Blues, r&b, rockabilly, western swing, swing blues, MoTown.

Good work, said Bryn's editor. *How did you hear about this band?* He was holding up her piece on something. An acid jazz-meets-qawwali duo, a Gypsy-chamber-folk quartet, a gamelan hip-hop ensemble.

Sometimes she saw a flyer. She read the bulletin boards outside health food stores, yoga studios, cafeterias and adult education classes. She read posters and email newsletters. She dropped by music classes and guitar stores. People recognized her, saved up tips and invites, told her about secret shows, house parties and art openings with arty combos that might grab her attention.

Every show that Bryn attended, she wrote up. She turned in the reviews in batches and the paper published some of them, but not all. The rest, Bryn began to self publish in a chapbook that she named *SetList*. At the end of each month, she gathered up her unpublished reviews, took the batch to Kinkos and ran off a hundred copies of *SetList*—it was usually a dozen pages or so—and stapled on a cover with an image taken from a crumpled and beer-stained set list that she snagged from the stage after a show one night.

At first, Bryn gave her chapbooks to her friends, and then she took to leaving them, a handful here and there, at the places that tipped her off about new bands. It was nothing, really. She typed her name on the cover of *SetList*, but she was no one. A girl with an unglamorous entry-level job at an unglamorous newspaper.

Months passed quietly. The sophomore slump reigned. And then. *And then.*

There's a guerrilla marching band performing next week, said the guy behind the counter of a secondhand book store. He wrote the address on the back of a receipt.

Thanks, said Bryn.

By the way, we ran out of your chapbooks and people have been asking for them. Can you drop off another batch?

She stared.

It is you, right? *SetList?*

She nodded.

Better print a double-batch, he said, and went back to the novel he had marked with his thumb.

The same scenario repeated itself a couple times. A few times. Then, with frequency.

You should charge for these, said Bryn's friend. Just a dollar.

No one will buy it.

I bet they will. And if they don't, you can always go back to free.

Bryn didn't want to do it, but paying for two hundred copies on her income was a stretch. She typed *$1 each* on the next batch and handed them uneasily to the bookstore clerk.

Cool, he shrugged, and when she returned, he took an envelope with her name from the drawer of the register. It had $50 inside.

I only gave you twenty-five copies, Bryn said.

I changed all the ones to twos, he said. So shoot me.

○

Ultimately, it was *SetList* that got the job. Bryn came along as its creator. She sat through the interview, pressing her fingers under her thighs to keep herself from twitching.

How did you get the idea for the chapbook? the interviewer asked.

(Novice question: What's your inspiration?)

Bryn edited out the part of the story that had to do with Spike, with his album, with his Swedish girlfriend. She didn't mention how the simple, mutual, clean break left her hollow and lost. She didn't mention the labyrinth or the sophomore slump.

She said, I love music. It's always been there for me. So I started looking for the kind of music that not so many people are there for. I wanted to go to those shows, and I wanted to tell other people about them.

Can you keep finding these quirky bands to write about?

Bryn nodded. I have good sources, she said.

Since she'd started printing her email address on the back of *SetList*, she'd been getting more and more tips. Bands asked her to come to their shows. People wrote to suggest their favorite underground acts. There was the occasional sting of a rude comment, but mostly the emails were requests for more reviews.

Have you ever had writer's block? asked the interviewer.

(A decent question. Maybe better would be: What have you learned from writer's block?

Or, *What does writer's block mean to you?*

Or, *Is writer's block real?)*

Bryan said, I haven't slowed down enough to think about writer's block. I listen and then I write what I hear. That's pretty much all there is to it. If I stopped listening to music, I guess I'd stop writing about it. But I don't see that happening. I write about music even when I don't get paid for it, so a job as a reviewer is only incentive.

The interviewer made a note on her tablet. She said they'd let Bryn know something by the end of the week. She held out her hand for a firm shake.

Two weeks later, Bryn was sitting at a new desk in front of a new computer.

She had graduated.

iv.

How did you get sober while you were on the road?

There's a long pause. The silence is cavernous. She thinks he's not going to answer, but she waits and just when she's given up, when she's about to say, *hey, don't worry about it. Don't answer that if you don't feel like it,* he answers.

He talks about what it was like going into the darkness. About the narcotic clutch of it, the welcoming fog. He talks about an African hallucinogen that lasted three days during which he thought of everything that was wrong with his life.

He talks of spiders, of skulls and boneyards and crypts. He talks of the visions, which still haunt him, and how he doesn't mind the haunting because the darkness was a familiar place.

He talks of the pale sickness that lasted and lasted, a sickness in his bones and in the cistern of his soul. And after that, a dreary dullness that blocked the sun and chilled him. He talks of wanting to go back, back to where things made sense in their carnival-of-horrors way, about how, when he could no longer stand the wanting to go back, he began to write about it. He turned the ache and burn and regret into poems, and he turned the poems into songs. He learned to live with a notebook in his pocket. If there was no paper, he wrote on his arms, on walls, on tabletops and in bathroom stalls.

You don't know what it was like, that long winter. That long journey across Siberia.

What?

He says, that's what I mean. You don't understand.

But she wants to. She wants to and it scares her. She wants to walk where he's walked, even into the roach-infested apartments, the single rooms with newspaper taped to the windows to block the light. She wants to go into the seedy bars, into the back rooms and bathrooms, into the alleys and lightless parks. She'd wait for him on stoops and benches, she'd hold his hair and clean the sick from his face, she'd wait for him to fall asleep and then to wake.

That's what she tells herself. That's what she believes.

But what kind of person would that make her? There's no room in her tightly-drawn life for an addict. There's no room for drama or problems or danger.

Why do the leaves change from the top of the tree down? He's asking, but she doesn't get the sense he's asking her. Maybe someone else is with him on his end of the line. He could be anywhere. On a bus, in a restaurant, in bed.

Why do the leaves change from the top of the tree down? It's like a koan of sorts. A poetic riddle. She writes it on down on her notepad and later, when he's talking about something else—about the audience in Paris, about the food in French truck stops (What they eat at truck stops is as good as what we eat in gourmet restaurants, he says), about his insomnia, about going home to the Midwest and seeing friends from high school—she underlines it. Twice.

Later, after the interview (maybe that night, or later that week, or some other time all together), she thinks about the two things he said.

You don't know what it was like, that long winter. And, *Why do the leaves change from the top of the tree down?*

She wonders if the two thoughts were not actually random at all, and if they weren't, what they mean.

She wonders why she told herself that she wanted to go where he'd gone, why she wanted to see what he'd been through. None of that was true. Even at her bravest she would never have walked into the sort apartment where a drug addict would…whatever.

The truth is, she can't allow herself to think of what he might have done.

The truth is that she's glad he's sober now, even if a sober rockstar might be less interesting than a rockstar who partakes.

That long journey across Siberia.

No, no I understand, she says to Jude.

You do?

I've spent a little time in Siberia. I've passed a long winter or two.

He can't see her tuck a strand of hair behind an ear. He says, then you know.

64

V.

Sometimes there's not enough silence. Sometimes there's not enough noise. It changes, week in and week out, the need for silence and the need for noise. There are days when Bryn sits at her desk with her headphones on, pretending to be listening to something, but in fact listening to nothing. Her own pulse in her ears.

Years ago, in high school, she'd done the same thing with her Walkman. Blocking out the clamor of the cafeteria with a headset. Sunglasses had a similar effect, creating a barrier between the self and the world. But a Walkman—pop on the headphones and even if the music wasn't playing, no one was likely to try to talk to her. She'd wear them on the bus, on the train, walking to school and, later, walking to work. Usually she'd listen to music, but the snug feeling of the headphones over her ears was a comfort of its own.

It *is* funny, when she thinks about it, that she ended up talking to people for a living. It's funny, until she hits a wall.

There are days, the days of silence, when Bryn doesn't think she can face speaking to anyone. Not even over the phone. Not even just for fifteen or twenty minutes. Not even if she coasts on her all-purpose questions.

- *Do you remember any of the questions you answered during your first interview?*
- *How do you measure success, and has that changed over the years?*
- *Do you remember what you wanted to be when you grew up?*
- *If you could go back and do your first album over, what would you do differently, and what do you think you got right?*
- *What has been the most surprising piece of advice you've received as a musician?*
- *What's the real story about groupies?*

Sometimes, before the call, Bryn puts her head down on the desk. She imagines crawling under the desk, into the dark cube usually reserved for her knees and the secret bottle of rum that she never touches but also never throws away.

Sometimes, before the call, Bryn gets up and walks briskly around the block. Sometimes she stretches, sometimes she drinks coffee. Sometimes she practices, in her head, being witty and charming.

*So, where are you today? Arizona? Is the heat really dry...*Oh crap. No, no, no.

Sometimes, more often than she'd like to admit, the thought rises in her mind that she can't do it. She can't make the call or take the call. She can't ask the questions or listen to the answers. She can't hold a conversation with a stranger. Especially not a famous stranger.

And then she lets go of all of that and picks up the phone. It works. But she still harbors the ember of fear that it won't always work. That one day her superpower (can talking to rockstars be considered a superpower?) will lose its potency.

○

During the silent times, life takes on a sort of glow. It doesn't shine and sparkle and burn hot like in the loud times, but it glows with its own internal light.

During the silent times, it's easy to pare back. Pare back to the basics, to the necessities in the lean times, and then when the fat times roll back around, even the slightest gain feels expansive. Luxurious.

Bryn passes through the grip of press, most of them men. Most of them paunchy, dressed in crumpled button-downs and Rockports. Most of them jockeying for good seats. Most of them, once the question and answer portion of the conference begins, asking long-winded questions that aren't really questions at all but statements about their own knowledge of music and the man to whom they're speaking.

Mr. Eno, I just want to say I'm a huge fan of Music For Airports. *I wrote my thesis about it; that and the concept of spatial music composed for large rooms in which groups of people are passing through. Your work has been such a huge inspiration to me and blah blah blah.*

Brian Eno, dressed all in black, has twinkling eyes set in a face that is not the same face he had as a young man, but he doesn't look old, either. He looks mischievous, ready to pop out of his chair and dart out of the room, onto something much more entertaining than answering press questions.

Mr. Eno, can you tell us about your influences?

Mr. Eno, can you tell us what medium you work in for your visual art?

Mr. Eno, what types of synthesizers are you currently working on?

Later, when the conference has been called to a close and the press mill around over bottles of beer, offering Brian Eno sweaty palms and shuffling off to type their notes into their laptops and iPads, Bryn makes her move.

Can I get you another drink? she asks.

He accepts.

A young guy in a shaggy beard and hoodie starts talking about production software. Brian Eno nods politely, names a few programs he's used, mostly listens to the guy until he's interrupted by a large camera lens.

Mr. Eno, a photo?

He nods, smiles, wraps an arm around Bryn's waist and pulls her into the frame. Immediately six other cameras are pointed at them.

When the room empties she says, I do have a question for you.

Let me guess. You want to know what Brian Ferry is *really* like.

Bryn laughs. No.

Good.

I'm wondering about your art. In your exhibit, the images keep changing and morphing, and the same combination will never be seen again. So how hard is it for you, as an artist, to relinquish control like that?

Brian Eno's eyes gleam. He talks about control and surrender. About how being able to exercise control is a wonderful quality of being human, but surrendering is a worthy practice.

He says, that's why we like art, because it takes us someplace else. That's why we like sex, that's why we like drugs and that's why we like religion. They're all forms of surrender.

Later, when she should be typing up her notes, Bryn thinks about that. Control versus surrender. She wishes she could have listened to Brian Eno talk about it longer, maybe over brandy. Maybe sitting in leather armchairs in front of a fire.

And then she thinks that she wants to talk to Jude Archer.

✪

Tell me about control and surrender. Because this is what I think: You're better at surrender. You know how to let go, into your art, into love, into drugs, into god.

69

—It's sex, not love.
What?
—The quote. He said, 'That's why we like sex.'
But I don't know about you and sex.
—Ah.

Bryn wakes from the ludicrousness of it. The conversation inside her head. She's embarrassed by how often she finds herself talking to Jude Archer in her mind. No one knows about it, but if they did, they'd think she was crazy. *She* thinks she's crazy. Who *does* that?

Okay, there's a reasonable explanation. She's readying herself for an interview. She's trying out her questions.

But why does he have to answer back?

He doesn't, of course. She's composing his answers for him.

In her weak moments she almost believes that he can hear her. Maybe not literally. Not like he's buttering his toast and then *poof*, there's her voice speaking into his mind, conducting the ongoing interview. But maybe they're connected. Maybe he can sense that there's someone out there thinking of him. Sending good energy his way.

Good energy? Really? Good grief.
Tell me about control. What do you control?
—My sobriety. My work.
And what do you surrender?
—You mean surrender into.
I do?
—You do.

Bryn shakes herself into the present again. She has work to do. Jude Archer may have taken up residence in her mind, but she can close the door to his room and refuse to pay him any attention. For the moment.

Part three

i.

There's a sort of grace period between realization and the end of innocence. The desire is to know, but once a person, a place, a thing is known, it can never be unknown. Before knowing but after becoming aware, there's an easy anticipation. The slide into summer vacation, the descent after a long flight, the hours before Christmas morning.

It was kind of like that, once the interview was set with Jude Archer. His publicist, Andrea, said, how about Thursday at eleven a.m.

Like it was no big deal. Like that's just what she did. Scheduled interviews.

Of course, that *is* just what she did.

But to Bryn it felt like the turn of a key.

✪

Bryn says, *Fly By Night* seems to be your most accessible. Do you think so, and if so, was that intentional?

I think so, he says. He sounds sleepy, close to the phone. He sounds like he's lying down, cradling the phone against his cheek. He tells Bryn that it's a breakup album.

I know that sounds cliché, he says, and she wonders how many other music writers he's told the same story to. But still she feels like it's only her. Like there's just the two of them.

He tells her there was a girl, that things ended badly. That he started writing his way through the separation, through the weeks and months of pulling *his* life out of what was once *their* life.

Bryn shoves her hair behind her ears and nods as if he can hear her nodding. She thinks that she's glad the girlfriend is out of the picture, and then she forces herself not to think that thought.

Jude says that by the time he went out to L.A., he had a couple dozen songs. The album was there, a rough draft culled from his heartache. He called on his friends on the West coast. He went into the studio and laid

73

down tracks. That's how it was done. Where there were holes, he wrote new songs to fill in the empty spaces.

He says, it's consistent because there was that theme.

It doesn't sound sad, though, she tells him.

I'm not sad anymore, he says.

Bryn says, so you go through this breakup and it inspires the songs for an album. But then you have to tour the album and revisit that raw emotion, night after night. Is that difficult, or do you transcend the pain?

There's silence on the other end of the phone, but Bryn knows it's a good question so she waits. She'll wait for Jude Archer, as long as it takes.

He comes back to her, says, it's not that anymore. I wrote the songs, and then I was done with it. The emotion wasn't mine anymore.

○

Fuck, fuck, fuck. Bryn tears off a sundress and throws it on the bed. A t-shirt that she used to think was cute but suddenly just looks desperate. A mini skirt. She's been telling herself for months, possibly years, that she needs to make an effort to dress up when she goes to shows. Especially if she's planning to meet someone. Even just in case she happens to meet someone. Not a date, a musician.

But none of this applies to meeting Jude Archer.

She finally drops the whole heap of discarded clothing into the laundry basket and puts on her same pair of black jeans that she's worn all day.

This is not how she envisioned it, not from the beginning. Not when the whole thing was just a vague idea and her imaginary wardrobe was expansive and effortlessly cool.

She did imagine it, though. More than she'd care to admit. Almost from the first time she listened to the album and began to conceive of an interview with Jude Archer and the opportunity to meet him in person, she was fantasizing what she'd wear, what she'd say. How she'd casually run her fingers through her hair, how she'd do something suave like hand him a mix CD of songs she'd burned (no, that would be dorky), or a book she'd picked out for him, or a poem that she'd written (again, no).

She'd let her mind go, sometimes, during long meetings and sometimes during even longer nights. She'd think about if he came into town early and had time before sound check and he'd call her and she'd meet him somewhere like a coffee shop and they'd spend the afternoon poking around antique stores or the cemetery, surprising each other with insights about life and art.

No, no, no. Way too corny.

But still, she thought it. And the thing was, how she imagined it could be, those few hours with Jude Archer, were so much better than the real relationships she was having with the people around her who were there every day.

In the end, it had to be jeans.

In the end, there weren't hours. No cemetery stroll, no CD mix, no hand-written poem.

Just Bryn in her jeans. Just Bryn.

✪

She says, you've flown under the radar—did you want fame? Do you feel fortunate to have not had major fame?

He laughs. There's an edge of bitterness. Says, of course I think I should be famous. With each album, I always think this is the one. And I think *Fly By Night* is the one.

I do, too, says Bryn.

Jude says, I don't fly under the radar because I'm trying to be cool or something. I wish I knew what it was that made some people take off, because I keep trying.

But you don't give up.

No, he says. He doesn't give up. He's thought about it, but then there's the next idea. He thinks it might be the last. He's not sure why he keeps going.

Momentum.

Yes.

I get that.

He says, the thing is, if I wasn't doing this, what would I be doing? Even if I wasn't making albums, I'd still be writing songs. I'd write poems and I'd paint paintings because that's what I do. It just comes out of me. So I'm glad I have an audience, even if I'm not getting rich, because at least there's someone to witness what I'm creating.

Someone to witness.

So tell me, Bryn says, when you start to work on an album, do you have a particular audience in mind? Are you writing for someone, or *to* someone?

He says, maybe. Sometimes.

Because it's a breakup album.

There's that.

But the rest of the time?

The question is, *When you make an album and put your work out there into the world, what do you hope to get back? Has that changed over the course of your career?* Bryn has it written on her scrap of paper. She's given the question a lot of thought, because it applies to her as well.

When you go into on an interview, what do you hope to get out of it?

The obvious answer, the correct answer, is a good story.

The also obvious but less correct answer is, connection. Approval, admiration, attention. But most of all connection. And not just with anyone. Connection with readers, yes, but more importantly with the rockstar.

To touch a star. That is something.

And, *Has that changed over the course of your career?*

Yes. And no.

✪

- Rule number 1: Listen more than you speak. Remember that this isn't about you, that your job is to extract answers, not dazzle with your knowledge and sparkling wit.
- Rule number 2: Do your research and ask good questions. And distill those questions to their essence for maximum impact and minimal wordiness (see Rule 1).
- Rule number 3: Built rapport, but don't try to win the rockstar as a friend. This is not about you, this is about your readers and their relationship with the rockstar. You are not on a date. You're not going to hang out. You're not going to become pen pals. No one is going to dedicate an album to you. Or remember your name five minutes after you hang up the phone.
- Rule number 4: There are no exceptions to Rule 3.

✪

Over the course of her career, Bryn has learned and relearned the truth

76

of the rules. She has stopped hoping for rockstar friendship, for the shout out from the stage, for the person on the other end of the line to *get* her.

But she can't stop wanting to be understood. She can't stop wanting to be seen as brilliant, important and unique by the very person who is, in her eyes, all of those things.

She still wants to touch a star. And the longer she works at it, the more she hones her skill, distills her questions, researches her subjects and cultivates true interest in them and their lives, the closer she gets to touching them. She can feel it.

Usually just feeling it is enough. With Jude Archer, her ache and longing to reach him clamors so loudly that she can barely hear him over the thud and jangle of her own nerves.

See me now.

She'll dream that scene. Him on the stage, leaning over a tangle of cables, his hair in his eyes.

See me now.

His eyes are wide-set, brown and flecked with gold. There's so much light behind them. He's lit from within. A candle. A torch raised to spite the dark.

See me now.

He looks up, focusing in the gloom of the club. And then he sees her. And then he smiles.

This is the difference between the music writer and the fan: Music writers cover artists even if they're not inspired to. It's about finding the one compelling element and following it. Unraveling it. Fans don't do that. For fans, it's simple: Love or hate. Fans go to the shows they like and don't bother with the rest.

Music writers try everything (music-wise). At least once. Probably several times.

Fans go to the concert, buy the t-shirt. Maybe they get a backstage pass and hang around long enough to take a photo with the rockstar. The photos look the same: Two people standing side-by-side, arms around each other's shoulders. The rockstar looks slightly tired, the fan is grinning. Usually someone in the frame is making devil fingers.

Writers go to the concert, try to blend in, take notes, leave as soon as the encore starts. A set list is worth more than an autograph. Even the best shows are work. But writers get to have real conversations with rockstars. Not just, *Great show.*

Not just, *I love your work. It's always meant a lot to me.*

But, *How do you feel about turning forty? What are your thoughts about aging in the music industry, which, at least in North America, is so youth-obsessed?*

Or, *Ten years out, in what ways has your career followed the path that you originally imagined when you first got into music?*

Or, *Is there something that you've wanted your albums to sound like or express or accomplish that has so far eluded you?*

And the writer gets to reach out to the publicists, who are—except for maybe road managers—often the closest thing to calling up the rockstar himself.

Jude's publicist, Andrea, wrote, *Hey Bryn, thanks for your interest in Jude and* Fly By Night. *He's just finishing up his first round of touring, but he's going back out on the road this fall, after the festivals are over. Why don't we set something up for then, okay?*

She signed it xo. Kiss, hug. [Rule number 3 addendum: You can assume a friendship with a publicist. A friendship can be mutually beneficial to you both. It may not be as ego-boosting as accomplishing friendship with a rockstar, but in real life it's not only more likely but more satisfying because publicists are pretty much just like you.]

○

Bryn twirls a pen and gazes at the blank page that refuses to manifest a list of her top five albums from the past year. The question isn't fair. Too general. Too based on assumption. (But what assumption? That everyone likes the same thing, more or less? That music writers speak for the general populace, only, like fortune tellers, they know sooner what is to be known?)

With widespread acceptance comes the ability of the masses to determine the meaning of a song. Whatever the original story was (from the artist who created the song, or the first listeners who dreamed its language of images and gestures into being), that is lost. What remains is a big picture. Often in the form of a commercial for cars or jeans.

So, what then? Is it better for a song to be more famous and farther reaching, but also more homogenized in its effect?

Or is it better for a song to languish in brilliant, meaningful obscurity?

And, sometimes, does fame enhance a song with importance? Can the adoration of millions shine a brighter light on a piece of art?

Bryn crumples the scrap of paper meant to list her top albums. Not that she needs to—it doesn't say anything—but the act of throwing it away gives her a sense of escape from the troubling question. She tears a new scrap from the back of a discarded envelope and jots the name of an experimental noise album from a solo musician. She jots the name of a collection of piano and synthesizer compositions whose first track makes her want to cry with nostalgia. She writes the name of an EP of French pop songs given to her by a musician who was passing through town. She knows she's being difficult, obstinate, a non-participator. But that's who she is.

○

She says, your songs have themes of running. Toward things and people, and away from them. I was wondering, do you literally run?

80

Like, am I a runner? asks Jude Archer.

Yes. Do you just like the words run and running, or do you actually go running?

He laughs: I used to run. I tell myself to get back into it. But no, I'm not a runner.

Maybe you should be. Maybe you're telling yourself to.

He says, I think about it, whenever I go on tour. I think I'll bring a pair of running shoes and start up again. But then I don't.

So maybe next time you will.

Maybe.

Sometimes, in the middle, the interview hits its stride. It's not about the questions or the answers, it's about a certain rhythm that gains its legs, and builds, and takes over.

Sometimes (most of the time, really), that doesn't happen. But when it does, Bryn does her best to lose herself in the ease of the moment.

There's a trick to that—finding the balance between floating and steering. An interview takes steering, but the magic comes from floating. It's a riddle of sorts.

○

Once, maybe twice or more, Bryn let her guard down in a face-to-face interview over a bottle of wine. His lips, Pinot-stained, formed words which her mind couldn't grasp.

Rockstar. White button-down with French cuffs left uncuffed, black combat boots left untied. Curly hair falling into wide eyes. Smudge of eyeliner. It was all too much, really, and what was he saying?

It's a breakup album. Sorry to sound so cliché, but it's true.

Fingers on tarnished silver cross, skull ring with a ruby in its eye socket. Heat of the room, of blood rushing to her face.

She sucked in her breath, smoothed her hair behind her ears.

Part of the trick is not to fall down the rabbit hole. Not to get caught up in the force field, but instead to jump into the deluge and tread water, keeping a level head in the current.

But that lovely mouth, those sleepy eyes, the tantalizing siren song of the alcohol. The low, glamorous lighting of the bar. The silky, sugary thought of how it would feel to be pressed between the body of this boy and the cool expanse of hotel sheets. It's just a flicker of a thought, more a body response, really. When the interview is happening, the nerves are rattling, and suddenly the low heat of the wine rises up the spine and the boy across the table (and wasn't he farther away just a few minutes ago? And does he smell of cedar and jasmine?) suddenly looks less like a subject and more like, well, a *boy.*

Don't go there. Let the hum of attraction propel the boat, but remain in the river, moving toward the destination. Do not go in for a swim, do not pull over to the side for a picnic. Do not go against the current, nor try to race the water. Drift, but remain alert. Wipe your sweaty palms on your thighs and order a glass of water.

❂

When the interview is coming to an end, Bryn is struck by the finality of it. Usually the home stretch is a relief. This time it almost hurts. She says at least three times, I know I've gone over our time.

Each time, he says, no, it's fine.

But finally it can't go on. Bryn thinks she could ask questions for days, but she already has so much more material than she can use. She says, well, thanks for talking. Thanks so much for your time.

He says, sure. I enjoyed it.

She says, me, too. Really. I know that's the polite thing to say, but I've looked forward to talking to you for weeks.

(Months, really. But he doesn't need to know that. Months sounds crazy.)

It's been nice talking to you, he says.

And I'm looking forward to your show, says Bryn.

Will you be there? Jude Archer asks her. As if he hasn't heard anything she's been saying. As if she'd be anywhere else.

Yes, I think so, she says casually.

Then come up and introduce yourself, he says. (They all say that. It's in the rockstar handbook.)

Bryn says, maybe, if you have time before your sound check, I could show you around town a little.

It takes an absurd amount of courage, and as soon as the words are out she worries that she sounds stupid. *Show you around town? Seriously?*

But Jude responds as if it's the most normal suggestion ever. Yeah, that sounds great. Or maybe we could get lunch. Just set it up with my road manager, okay?

Okay, says Bryn. And even when he hangs up, she sits there for a few seconds with the receiver pressed against her ear, listening to the static of the dead line.

Just a few seconds. Maybe half a minute. Not long enough for anyone to notice.

Skinny.

Dirty jeans from how many days, weeks of wear? Dirty hair, or hair made to look dirty. Palmed through with dirty hands, or hands that are not dirty but are decorated with the trappings of the world. Wrists of leather cords, studded cuffs, skull beads. Fingernails painted black and the polish chipped and cracked. A silver skull ring, or a silver snake wrapped up a long finger.

Hair cut by a band mate or a girlfriend, or perhaps cut expensively by a stylist, but cut to look uncut. Shaggy, falling over eyes and tucked behind an ear to reveal a gleaming stud or a silver hoop. Hair that looks slept in and lived in but somehow, up close, smells of incense and macadamia oil. Something exotic and dark.

Wood. Forest. Nightfall. Far away places. Escape. Dreams.

Jeans, battered and frayed. Muscled into shape, the stiffness of denim worn soft and smooth. Made to fit the body, made to do the bidding of a life.

Roads, train stations, takeoffs and landings. Waiting. Waiting rooms and lounges, bus seats, small compartments not really made for sleeping and yet somehow sleep comes.

Or else sleep doesn't come, and dreamlessness leaves its mark in the shadows and lines of the face. Dreamlessness, or the extended dream state, or the long reach of insomnia—they all play their part in the process of how songs come into being. Lulled, cajoled, wrestled, battled, pleaded, dared, prayed for.

Or just ignored. Ignored into being.

Sometimes all the things are just talismans. The jewelry, the tattoos, the hair, the denim. Just accoutrements of and distractions from the real thing, which is the song.

Sometimes, like prayer, calling out to a talisman is just as good as calling out to whatever stone-deaf and preoccupied deity is supposed to hear the prayer in the first place. Just call out to something, to anything. Just go through the motions of calling.

Whatever the motions. Get on your knees. Fold your hands. Step out on stage. Walk to a crossroads in a rural Southern town. Just show up somewhere and ask for the thing.

Dare yourself to say the thing.

The thing that you want.

The thing that once had a name and now is too big, too consuming, too woven into the fabric of living and dreaming to name anymore.

Or, stop naming the thing and simply become it. Put on the jeans, the studded cuff, the silver hoop. Tattoo it onto your skin, drink it into your guts, breathe it into your lungs. Cut your hair just so and paint your eyes and then step out on stage and do your very best impression. Act the part until you lose track of the point where you end and the character begins.

And then you can begin in earnest.

Strip yourself of flesh and artifice. Starve out the rest. Or drown it in drink. Or run from it.

Lay everything at the altar of becoming. Or lay nothing. Stand in the wings, in the dark, miles and lifetimes from the spotlight and grab for the sparkle that comes out of the nothing. Collect the glitter and stardust that hangs in the air. The discarded shine, the remnants, the castoffs, the glinting dust of the universe that is yours.

Sew yourself a mantle and cloak yourself in glitter until you're indecipherable from the stars.

And then you have arrived.

❂

When Bryn was in high school she wasn't cool. She knew that at the time. What she didn't know was that cool was a moving target and ten, fifteen, twenty years out she'd look back at her sixteen-year-old self and see the cool that she'd never felt at the time. The sulky, brooding girl in fingerless gloves.

The thing that she learned over the years of interviewing rockstars was that some of them were cool in high school and some were complete outcasts. But all of them eventually discovered an inner light.

Not light like spirituality or whatever. Maybe that, but not necessarily. More of a shine, a magnetism. Cool isn't something that can be quantified or defined. There's no absolute formula. For each person it's something different.

Aloofness. Individuality. Daring. Intelligence. Wit. Style. Speed. Cleverness. Badassedness. Mysteriousness. Chic. Talent. Class. Deviousness. Suave.

But whatever the ingredients, no one ever became a rockstar without the end result. That impossible-to-put-a-finger-on combination of elements that adds up to undeniable cool.

○

After the interview, after the story is filed, there's a lull. Not in Bryn's workload, but in the build of excitement and the momentum toward Jude Archer. Without him, his voice, the conversation on the horizon, everything else seems dull.

Bryn feels herself fade a bit, and she fights the impulse to believe that the fading is happening. How many people have fallen victim to that kind of magical thinking? That someone out there illuminates you, brightens your world, points to what is golden and shining. And that same person can turn off the light.

How can Jude Archer have his finger on the switch?

He can't, Bryn tells herself. And she does her best to go back to being the way she once was, in those dim days before Jude Archer emerged from the sonic ethers.

It's not that going back is a bad thing. It's as comfortable as a pair of jeans and a sweatshirt—but it's stepping into that soft, familiar uniform after spending time in couture and reaping the attention and glamour that goes along with high style. To return, like Cinderella, to the apparel of the ordinary almost hurts.

Bryn does her work. She meets friends at bars. She goes to shows. She thinks about a vacation, signs up for a class in conversational French and makes a hair appointment. Life takes on a muffled quality that is hard to object to.

And yet. Just beyond that periphery of duty and routine is a glimmer of excitement. An unpredictable land of adrenaline and adventure. It's the shine of the city as glimpsed from the low-lit suburbs.

iv.

The time for load in comes and goes with no text telling her she can head over. Bryn's heart rattles. She made the mistake of drinking an iced Americano and the caffeine swirls devilishly through her blood. She pours a glass of water and it sloshes in her shaky hand. She packs up her work for the day, tries to act casual.

Are you going to get to meet him? Andrea asks in an email.

Bryn replies, probably. I might try to catch sound check.

She turns off her computer and walks out of the office like she's taking an afternoon stroll.

The time in between—driving to her house, parking, unlocking the door, setting down her things and stripping off her work clothes—is interminable. Minutes drip.

Bryn puts on music. She hyperventilates her way into a pair of skinny jeans and a t-shirt.

She throws a few things into a clutch. Chapstick, keys, credit card, license. She checks her phone again. Still nothing from the tour manager, but surely they're at the club. She takes a deep breath and gets back into her car.

And then, on the way there, something shifts. The anxiety floats away and is replaced with a cool clarity. *Pay attention to this moment. These are the last moments of Jude Archer existing only in your mind. Five more minutes and you can never have that back.*

(See the like/dislike-to-band/musician ratio rules, scenario 6: There is no chance of maintaining the same level of like or dislike. Meeting a musician in person changes everything.)

Bryn drives past the club. There's a van in front with its back door open wide. Of course that's his. Of course it is. She parks on the street and walks back. It gives her a moment to straighten her shirt and wipe the smeared mascara from under her eyes. Ease a lock of hair behind an ear. Think about thinking of nothing.

Just be yourself, she thinks. *That's all that's left to do.* All these weeks and months of waiting and planning, of lining up circumstances and orchestrating moments. Nothing's left but to show up and let the universe have its way.

And then she's inside the dark and mostly-empty club, its floors clean swept and its doors flung open to let the cool air rinse the smell of sour beer and bodies. There's music, too. She knows the sound. Jude Archer is barefoot on stage.

He looks just like he always looks in every video and photograph.

Later, sitting next to him on the edge of the stage, Bryn notices the tattoos that climb his arms. A jungle of skeletal faces, vines, stars. Things that have meaning to him alone. She notices that his eyes are sleepy, set wide in his face. When he looks right at her, which is only a couple of times, those eyes burn.

He rifles through a box of art supplies, looking for something, pulling out a paint-hardened brush. This is what happens when you don't wash your brushes, he says.

Yeah, I think that one's done for, Bryn says, pulling her knees up to her chest.

You can keep it, Jude says, holding it out to her.

She pauses. *Um, really? Is he joking? Does he think I want his trashed brush? Is that how it is with fans?* She wouldn't make a good fan.

He takes it back, finds a paint marker in his art box and begins to draw something. It's a skinny figure stretching the length of the handle, its one large orb of an eye gazing upward to a star that Jude draws on the stiff bristles. That's the star of hope, he says. There's a tired little boy inside his voice.

I like it, Bryn says.

I'll sign it, he says, and on the back he writes, *To Bryn with love, Jude A.* This time, when he hands it to her, she takes it.

Bryn wants to say the right thing, but what? *I love it. I'll treasure it. I'll hang it on my wall...* She settles on thank you.

Jude nods, says, I have to go lay down for thirty minutes.

Like that, their time is done. Fifteen minutes and a piece of art on a paintbrush. Bryn hands him a wrapped book. It's for your birthday, she says.

Am I supposed to wait until then to open it? he asks. He's the boy again.

Bryn says, it's your gift. You can open it whenever you want.

He tears the paper off and looks at it, smoothing his hand over the yellowed cover of Charles Johnson's *Faith and the Good Thing*.

It's from the '70s, she says.

Did you read it? Jude asks.

I did. Years ago.

Is it good?

I think you'll get it.

He seems satisfied with that answer, leaning forward and kissing her on the cheek. Says, okay. I'll see you in a little while.

And that's it.

❂

It feels like the most important part is sitting with Jude at the edge of the stage. Hanging onto his few words, the space in between words, plumbing silence for meaning.

But really, the most important part is in the minutes before arriving.

Pay attention to this moment. These are the last moments of Jude Archer existing only in your mind. Five more minutes and you can never have that back.

To become the girl who talks to rockstars was a journey, and Bryn its most unlikely adventurer. She was the girl who could barely raise her voice to audible when called on in class, the girl who would never try out for a school musical, who would shrink in fear from a microphone.

She was the girl who no one asked to dance, let alone asked to the prom. But, she *was* the girl who was kissed in the dark corner under the bleachers while everyone else made slow revolutions to REO Speedwagon. She was the unlikely crush, the curiosity.

And then, almost a turn-on-a-dime moment, Bryn changed from not-yet-having-bloomed into girlfriend material, to being beyond the statute of limitations. Her awkward, bony-kneed, smudged-mascara-ed youth merged into the fully-grown years of a thin, sharp, smart woman with a smudged-mascara specter just behind her smile.

Tethered men glanced her way on the train, in the streets. The boys who'd barely noticed her in high school began to look her up on Facebook, writing curious notes—*I always thought you'd do something interesting with your life.* And, *Is it true you met Chris Cornell?*

They wrote their notes from the bland safety of their split-levels and suburban lives while their families slept.

91

Bryn felt herself as they saw her. An anomaly, an exotic defector from their own familiar world.

But she was beyond them. Beyond the ordinary lives of the men who hadn't wanted her when she was willing to be indicted into ordinariness. Beyond the everydayness of conversations, or expectations, or desires.

In the years since Bryn had allowed her kisses to be stolen under the bleachers, she had evolved into an outsider of her own design. She had navigated a strange world and found her niche there. She had learned a new language and in that language she spoke to rockstars.

But she couldn't lose herself to speaking to Jude. Even if all of this, all of these years and all of this work, was just preparation for a single conversation on the edge of a stage.

She saw it in the moment. She saw herself leaning toward Jude Archer, running toward him. But she also saw herself stopping short, drawing back, composing herself again.

Even if all of this was just to reach this particular musician in this particular minute, did that mean she had to stay the course? Or could she take the momentum and turn it into something new, into the next thing?

Because *that* was what she wanted, right?

○

While Jude sleeps in his van, Bryn sits on a bar stool and orders a sandwich. She chats with the bartender and chats with the guy on the next barstool. She resists the urge to look over her shoulder every few minutes to see if Jude has emerged. If, perhaps, he's looking for her.

It has to be enough. The one conversation. The paintbrush signed to her. The awkwardness of it all, the way none of it was the way she'd imagined.

Because, in imagination, everything is smooth and soft around the edges. There are no bizarre, blurted phrases. No uncomfortable silences. No misunderstandings.

In real life, sitting on the stage with Jude, everything was weighty and strange. The ease and warmth of the phone interview had given way to a meeting of strangers with little immediate chemistry to lessen their strangeness.

You have to admit that to yourself, right?
Wrong.

Bryn talks to the guy on the next barstool about music. About Jude's music. About how important *Fly By Night* is to him and how he's taken his vacation days so that he can follow Jude's tour for a week. This is the first show.

Bryn's instantly jealous. Tour. A week of shows. A week of chances to redo the conversation at the edge of the stage. But that's not her role. Her role is to be the interviewer. Her job ends before the show even begins. All of this—load in, sound check, hanging out in a mostly-empty bar an hour before a concert begins—all of it is uncharted territory.

V.

Later, Bryn won't think about how she willed herself to stay after the show had ended. After Jude had played his last song and then an encore and then, when the crowd kept clapping, promised to play another song, unplugged, at the merch booth.

He did exactly that, perched on a stool, folding his tall frame over his guitar. The audience remained in a tight semi-circle around the display of collectible vinyl albums and t-shirts that Jude had designed. He sang into the hush of the lobby, making the space ring with his voice. And when he was done, he stayed on his stool, signing CD covers and shaking hands, his voice low and sleepy as always, bouncing against the night.

Bryn's instinct was to leave then. To be absorbed by the crowd and swept out the door. Enough had happened. She'd remember it, the whole evening stretching out like a book of snapshots.

Instead, she resisted the urge to flee and hung back, talking to the pretty blond merch girl who was traveling in the van with Jude and his road manager.

I'm Eva, said the girl. I'm only with the tour until Austin.

She couldn't be older than twenty-two, her wardrobe a luxe hippy collection of long necklaces, a skimpy sundress and tall boots.

But Bryn liked her, felt the ease around Eva that she didn't feel earlier with Jude.

As the crowd thinned and the t-shirt sales slowed, Jude's road manager, Zack, edged into the conversation with Bryn and Eva. They talked about playing Atlanta and Nashville. They talked about road food and placed bets on who would get up in time for breakfast at the B&B where they were spending the night.

Bryn felt like an insider, pulled into a circle that she'd never been in before. She had talked to bands after shows, but not to the crew. And when Jude finally ambled over, he treated Bryn differently. Like she was part of the road family.

Thanks for the article, he said.

Oh, it was no problem.

No, really, he said. It was good.

Bryn nudged his ribs. Said, you don't have to say that. Andrea told me that you don't read press.

But I read yours, he said.

Bryn flushed, felt pleased and confused, shoved her hair back behind her ears. She tried to hide her embarrassment by turning to the merch, which Eva was in the process of packing away.

She said, I was thinking, I should do this someday. Go on tour, sell t-shirts or something. Just so I can travel with a band for awhile and see what it's like behind the scenes.

You should, said Jude. He looked serious.

I figured it might help my writing.

He told her about the tour, about the difference between playing solo shows and being on stage at a festival over the summer. He jumped subjects, talked about selling his art, about how he learned that he had to ask for at least $500 for each painting.

Zack returned and said they should load up. Early start in the morning to get to the next show.

Bryn wondered if they'd invite her to wherever they went after the bar. Out for food? Back to the B&B? But no. There was no invitation.

Bryn said, if you go out for breakfast, text me and let me know. I'd like to meet you.

Zack said he would. Of course, he didn't ever text about load in, but Bryn had to hope. Asking meant the possibility was there. The night was done but Jude Archer hadn't yet passed through her fingers.

I'd like to keep in touch, she said to Jude, flipping her hand uselessly. I know that sounds—

There's Facebook, he said, as if that was a natural thing to say. As if he read his mail. As if he'd write back.

Jude bent a little to hug her. When they parted, something of him clung to her. Not his scent, exactly, but the aura of his scent. The specter of him, which haunted her through the parking lot and into her car where she buckled herself in and pulled onto the road before she began to cry.

The tears came as a surprise. Maybe a relief. Heavy sobs culled up from her stomach, shaking her. She was glad for the dark, for the empty streets, for the occasional blown-out streetlight giving her some privacy in her inexplicable grief.

But why grief? Why now?

It was because, with that last hug, she found what she'd known was there. She knew that Jude Archer was a part of her, but she couldn't explain what part or in what way, and she knew that if she did happen to see him again in the morning, it could be the last time. At best, he'd come through town on tour once a year. A year wasn't often enough to see someone so important.

She knew all of that, and as much as she felt contained in the knowledge, Bryn also found herself at the edge of a new understanding: That she really knew *nothing*.

She could try to keep in touch with Jude, maintain a friendship through email. And he wouldn't write back. That was logical. Only she didn't really *know* that it would happen like that. She was simply guessing.

She believed that what she felt was hers alone. That her importance in Jude's world was nothing. But she didn't know that for certain, either. And she didn't know what the future held. Or, how to go on with all of that not knowing.

Except that not knowing was not the same as uncertainty. It was not the same as walking blind. It was more like remaining open to the potential of things to come.

○

It's a day of bright sun. Maybe Indian summer, maybe one of those days in winter when the sky is achingly blue and it's not important that the branches are bare and that by dusk the air will turn chilly. The height of the day is maniacally perfect, and for a few hours, nothing else matters.

(Why do the leaves change from the top of the tree down?)

It's kind of like being day drunk, without the lethargy, the hangover and the guilt that follows.

How many of those days have there been? How many does one person get? Hard to say. Perhaps harder even to count them, because each one is unexpected, unplanned, fleeting.

Maybe it's the fleetingness that makes those days so special. An escape from the ordinary. A shaking of the pieces; life in a snow globe.

○

In the morning, Bryn is fine. Calm. Even relaxed. She dresses carefully, checks herself in the mirror. At work, she sits at her desk and goes through the motions but as the minutes and then hours pass the calm fades and she's increasingly aware of the clock.

It's an albatross.

Finally, at noon, she realizes they must have left. They have a five hour drive before load in at the next town. Surely they're on the road. And why did she think anyone would call her?

There's some relief in knowing it's all done.

But then her phone does ring. It's Zack and he says they've finally packed the van and does she want to meet them for coffee somewhere.

Yes, sure, of course. Bryn gives directions to a place. She checks her hair, grabs her jacket and flees the office. Everything is open again, and loose, and free. The air is electric as she strides through town. Buildings and windows have a shine. Colors are clean-washed.

And then Bryn is walking into the coffee shop and everyone is there. Eva and Zack and Jude. They pull her in, hug her one at a time, greet her with a familiarity beyond the few hours they've all spent in the same room.

Eva is wearing a Mr. Rogers t-shirt with the collar cut low. All three of them are wearing ironic t-shirts: Zack has a Wham! concert tour shirt and Jude has a Kiss Me I'm Irish shirt. Bryn feels overly serious in her outfit, like the only adult among teenagers.

But they treat her like their own, chattering about the B&B and where they'll stay next, telling Bryn about a collection of outsider art they visited the day before, and how they'd been listening to standup comedy in the van, how Jude had installed Sirius radio before the trip.

There's no mention of shows or songs. No talk of Jude playing *Austin City Limits* in a few days. Just the giggling banter of kids on a road trip.

Bryn watches Eva, who is young and beautiful. Beautiful despite her youth. Bryn can't help but wonder if Eva and Jude will get together on the trip. So much time spent together in close quarters and no one else to talk to. How could it *not* happen?

And doesn't Jude's next album depend on it?

Bryn searches herself for the burn of jealousy and comes up empty. Jude is looking at her.

What?

I asked if you wanted to see the piece of art I bought.

Of course I do, she says.

It's in the van.

Zack says, don't go. That's how we lure you in. Jude talks you into seeing his art, and then Eva knocks you over the head and we take you on tour with us.

Bryn laughs, finds herself shrugging. *Okay, sure. Do it now. I won't argue.*

You *should* come with us, says Jude. Sleepy eyes. He runs a palm over his hair.

Bryn wants the invitation to be real, but of course it isn't. It's real enough for her to play along. Not real enough that they would wait for her to pack a bag.

The coffee cools. The day edges into afternoon. It's almost enough. It has to be enough.

In daylight, Jude Archer is still larger than life. He eats a muffin, folding the paper into a tight square and complaining that he wants another but he can't have one or he'll get fat. All of the riding in the van.

Time passes, but no one seems to be in a hurry. Bryn can feel her own harried rhythm shift and slow into theirs. It's all lengths of time stretching across hours and miles. It's all moving and waiting.

Zack finally stirs from his newspaper. We'll already be late for load in, he says.

Right before they all leave, Bryn will hand her camera to Eva and ask for a picture with Jude. Jude will put his arm around Bryn's waist and Bryn will feel slightly disappointed because she saw him strike this same pose over and over after his show. But his body is warm and solid against hers and he'll keep standing there, telling Eva, I was smiling too much, take it again.

Later, Bryn will upload the photos to her computer and in all of them, Jude is smiling wide and open. Beside him, nestled into the crook of his elbow, Bryn looks somber. Just the tiniest smirk at the corner of her mouth. It's not fair that the photo doesn't do justice to the complex brew of emotions and ideas swirling around the moment.

Zack pulls the van around. Eva gives Bryn a quick hug and says, See you soon! which is sweet even though it's unlikely.

Then it's just Bryn and Jude standing by the side of the road.

Email me, he says.

Okay.

He pulls her in, wrapping her in both arms. She thinks that when he's gone, it will hurt.

And then he's in the van and they're pulling out, moving toward the highway. Bryn watches them go, waving and then not waving. Just watching.

○

An interview is two things: A fact-finding mission and a story-telling venture in which both parties agree to treat the story as truth. Being the writer means being the perpetrator of the myth—being its champion, its designer, its collaborator. The writer is implicit, an accessory to the crime.

Rockstars are mythological creatures brought to life. A rockstar is the point where a carefully contrived fiction fuses with an actual person. A person with a talent, a wardrobe and a dream (all of which he or she wants to keep); a person with a past, a family and a particular set of scars (all of which he or she wants to leave far, far behind).

But rockstars are also self-made superheroes. Peter Parkers turned into Spidermen because there comes a point when there's nothing left to do but climb the walls.

What Bryn always wanted was to be part of the fiction. She's willing to be the getaway driver because, even though she was never going to be the one on stage, helping to secure the spotlight for other rockstars-in-the-making also sealed Bryn's own fiction. Her own narrative about how she left behind a shy girl in a small town and became someone with a voice.

Whatever.

Suddenly there's a new story. The story behind the fiction. The back story. The deeper story, with its shadows and its bruises. Its failures, its sour notes, its nuclear winters.

○

So, if I tell you something, you promise not to laugh?
No.
Then I won't tell you.
What difference does it make if I laugh? I like to laugh.
Fine. You know, I thought you'd be so much cooler.
Ha. See? I'm totally laughing.
That's not the thing.
Oh, that's not the thing? You just thought you'd come off with, I thought

you'd be so much cooler?

No. Yes. I was just letting you know.

I never said I was cool.

You didn't have to say it.

What?

I mean, you just give off that vibe. What you do, how you are, the way you talk, the songs you write.

No, you're wrong. I'm the jerk with his heart on his sleeve. I'm a sap. I write songs that girls like.

Who said that?

Probably you.

I never said that.

Maybe you just thought it. Really loudly.

It's in your job description to be cool.

I don't have a job description. I don't even have a job. I just do what I do, and I try to be honest.

Honesty is so…

So not cool?

Kind of.

It doesn't matter, you know. It's not like you can measure what's cool. It's a moving target. Might as well keep on taking shots, right?

You're right.

Of course I'm right.

Don't get cocky.

Then tell what you were going to tell me. I'm waiting.

Well…

Tell me. I won't laugh.

Okay.

Part four

There's a hard edge to the day. The sky is steel grey; it's chilly without being cold. Indoors isn't any better than outdoors—the office radiators don't come on and the overhead lights barely cut the gloom.

The other writers sit at their desks tapping away on their keyboards, but Bryn can't focus. She drops her headphones over her ears and cranks up the Black Keys, blasting the lonely echo with the fullness of noise. Guitar and drums. Pummeling drums.

✪

She sits across from him in the café and steels her emotions. And then she wonders why she's doing that, why she doesn't just let it all out. Just this once. All of this practice in professionalism, all of these years of learning the rules, refining the rules and following the rules—if it's all led to right here, then what? What was it all for?

Is she going backward or forward? Is she regressing, returning to the girl she was when she was young and lonely? That girl, in her black nail polish and fingerless gloves, the girl kissed under the bleachers and slow danced with in secret. The girl who would do anything to feel something beyond lonely and bored. The girl who was just a girl, dreaming of being an adult, pressing her very being forward into the future.

And now. The woman of now, who still feels like a sixteen year-old girl, and who still feels lonely but only in the rare moments when she quiets her mind and lets down her guard.

The rules make life run smoothly, but they also barricade against loneliness. The rules are a wall between goals and pathless moments like these.

He says, sometimes when you look at me, I feel like you're seeing right through me.

He leans back in his chair, not all that bothered by being seen through.

She thinks that he's absurd, and that he's lovely. She can imagine the feel of his hair against her fingertips, she can almost feel the gravitational pull calling her hand to his head, her fingers knotting in that hair and bringing his face close to hers over the table.

She doesn't do this.

She leans back, too. Cools her heart. Says, oh, don't be ridiculous. I can't see through you.

But she can. She knows enough to know that if she stays cool, keeps it together, doesn't ask anything of him, she can hold him here with her. Close, but not touching. Wanting but not having. Arriving. Always arriving.

✪

What about the one-hit wonders? The one-album wonders? They, too, left their sweat on stages and their blood on drum skins. They stood in spotlights and then faded out of sight. To where? To smaller labels, to bigger disasters, to life.

Young Marble Giants, The Sex Pistols, The La's.

Bryn wonders, sometimes, if it's wrong to mourn their passing. The passing is inevitable—it's the ones who don't pass who are the exceptions to the rule. But still. Their songs remain even after they've vanished from memory.

✪

He's easy in his skin. Even as he folds his body to fit in the tight corner of the café, he looks at ease. He laughs easily, no shadow passing across his eyes. It's as if the hard edges of being human—the bruised hearts, broken bones, crushed dreams and rejection letters—never found their way to him.

But of course they have. If anything, he's been more broken, more soiled, more shattered, more battered, more left for dead.

He rises like a man made of smoke, like a body inhabited by a ghost of smoke, like the rounded, white breath of winter without the cold sting. He rises like the slow bubbles of vinho verde, effervescent but unhurried. His eyes turn up for just a moment, distant but warm.

He's the dweller on the threshold, and he is the threshold. He's the doorway between worlds. He says, I don't regret anything.

✪

Bryn stops herself from thinking. He can live in her heart if he must, but only in one room and behind a closed door. She can't go on like this, spending her days thinking of him, replaying all the things that did and did not happen. That isn't living, is it? It's a form of mourning, returning over and over to the past.

So she folds him into a small corner of herself and begins the work of forgetting. It's not hard work. In a way, it's the absence of work. But there is effort involved. The effort of not thinking, not dreaming, not recalling. Not speaking his name, not searching for his photo, not listening to his songs.

Bryn takes comfort in the thought that what she's forgetting is only her own imaginings, her own perceptions and projections of a moment that was fleeting at best. There's nothing tangible to hang on to. Well, the paintbrush. But even that is out of sight on a high shelf, slowly succumbing to dust.

○

Hi Jude,

This is me, keeping in touch. Wondering how your tour is going and if you're able to get any sleep. I think you have like five thousand women following your every status update and progress report, offering to look after you and tuck you in at night. So you're not getting that from me. Just this little note.

Be well,

B.

○

The girl, Lacey, came into the office once before for an interview and now she's back. She waits in the hall with her mother and if Bryn hadn't been expecting her, she never would have recognized Lacey.

It's been a year and a half, which for many people is a short time. But even though this is Lacey's second album that she's come to talk about, she's only seventeen. Still in high school.

Lacey's mother hangs nervously in the doorway even after Bryn invites her to sit. She asks, should I? Should I come in?

You're welcome to, says Bryn, who wants to squirm in the awkwardness of this family dynamic.

No, I'll only make her mad, says the mother. I'll just wait outside until she's done.

She darts away and Lacey sinks tiredly into a chair.

Bryn turns on the recorder, unfolds and refolds her questions, decides to abandon them and just talk to the girl. She can remember, with sudden clarity, her first interview with Lacey and understanding that this girl wasn't a young musician as much as a child. A tenth grader at the time, precocious and talented. Overly enthusiastic.

Now, propping her chin up on her palm, Lacey looks weary.

She announces, I'm not going to college right away. It's been an ongoing battle with my parents.

They want you to go? Bryn asks.

Lacey nods.

What do you want to do?

Go on tour in Europe. I'm already working on setting it up.

That doesn't sound like a bad idea, Bryn tells her, and Lacey looks grateful.

All of the questions, the ones on the scrap of paper and the ones hanging in the air, waiting to be asked, are about the construction of the songs. The strange play between dark imagery and bubbly pop melodies. The many references, some obvious and other buried, to hurt and love lost.

Lacey says, I just want to say something that people can relate to. I want it to sound light, so if you're not really listening it's no big deal. But if you do pay attention, then there's something more there.

She lifts her hand to sweep her bangs from her eyes. She's wearing short sleeves, and her forearm is striped with pale scars.

Bryn stills her face, slides her eyes to the side. One of the songs is called Hospital Room. One is called Bleed. The question that remains is no longer a question but an elephant, and Bryn wants to say *tell me. Tell someone.*

Instead she says, tell me some of the things that have happened in your life in the past year to inspire this new collection of songs.

Lacey talks of switching schools, of first love, of the sadness of leaving childhood. It all sounds scripted. She speaks in carefully formed words while vacantly tracing her fingertips over the topography of scars.

She says, the whole time you're in high school, it's like you're half a person. You have rights and you can make choices, but only certain choices. And now I'm almost free to really be myself and be in the world.

It's possible that the world will swallow her. It's possible that she'll find her way and walk out of whatever darkness she's been living in. Bryn wishes she could write the end of that story, see it to a good place.

But stories want to tell themselves.

○

The beginning is rarely where it seems like it should be. Lacey's problem, Bryn's career, the point where uncoolness gives way to coolness, the divide between not knowing Jude Archer and knowing him.

You should email him, says Andrea. Really. He'd love it.

But Bryn can't. Not now. She lives in the space without him, the dreary days leading up to winter. Days of crows. Days of early dark and rapidly-vanishing twilight.

She walks home from work in the clutch of darkness. In the distance, the lights of houses sparkle on black hillsides. The sight always reminds Bryn of a children's story about the gnomes who live in the hills mining gems. In the story, the insides of mountains are secret worlds lit by internal fires and the flash of gold and diamonds.

She would tell Jude about this. She'd talk to him of the mundane, and of the shimmer just beyond the known world where the unknown waits to be discovered.

Or doesn't wait. Just goes on as it always has, unaware that it has to be found.

The unfound doesn't necessarily feel lost.

A mouth unkissed doesn't register the lack until the kiss has come and gone and left its indelible mark. And the ghost of its mark. It's in the absence that the presence is most felt and most missed.

But there's no real kiss from Jude Archer to miss (does a cheek count?)—so why is it that the brush of his lips, the shadow of his voice in her ear, the glance of his touch all haunt her? Why is it that when she pulls the heavy comforter over her at night, it's his body that for a moment seems to pin her to the bed?

This is not a love story: Longing has no place here.

Bryn plays other music while she walks—The Love Language, Yann Tiersen, vintage Rolling Stones. Whatever. Whatever it takes. Music to set a pace, music to keep one foot in front of another, music to override the cascade of images that taunt the mind's eye.

○

107

If you're listening, if you feel me, too, then you should know I think of you when I'm in between places. When I'm outside, looking into the warm-lit boxes of other people's lives, and feeling the chill but not minding. You could find me here, if you wanted me.

Of course you're not listening. We're not connected. We're not clairvoyant.

If we were clairvoyant—if you were—then you'd hear me all the time, talking to you more than is reasonable. Is there any amount of talking to you within the confines of my mind that could possibly be reasonable?

So I'm glad you don't know that I do this. I'm glad you don't know that I'm lonely.

But is loneliness really weakness? I'm not out here because I have nowhere to go or no one to be with. I'd just rather be alone with my thoughts of you for now.

✪

Jude,

Do you think the world will end? Eventually will one of these Doomsday nutcases get it right? Or does it just go on and on, despite our weak and limited minds that insist upon imagining our own demise?

And are these questions even worth asking? I sometimes think asking the right question is more important than getting the right answer.

B.

ii.

This is the edge of the known universe, even though it looks like what has always been.

Bryn goes to work, types notes, listens to albums. There's a rhythm to the day. She writes a story, takes a call, buys a sandwich. Things tick, move forward. Time is measured in fractions. The ache is lost to the pulse of it all: the tides, the trains, the turnstiles. What was once a sonnet is pared back to a haiku, but it's no less musical.

And then something happens. The next rockstar says, if you come to the show, make sure you come up and say hello.

Bryn says, of course I will, like she always does. And then she goes to the show and makes a point of going up to say hello. Like she *never* does.

There's always been a separation—get to know them before the interview. Find the point of connection, get as close as words allow. And then let go, move on. Walk away unscathed.

Only now Bryn wants to be scathed. Nothing is as it once was. There's no more proving a point, no more fighting her way up to the best job. No more making Preston Schott sorry.

There's only this desire to take the next step into knowing.

She says, hello. I'm Bryn. I interviewed you.

He says, oh yeah. Thanks for that. He's Mars Taylor. Red hair and blue eyes.

It's my job, Bryn says.

They smile at each other awkwardly. On stage he's all energy and exuberance. In person he's smaller, slightly nervous.

Bryn tells him how she likes his songwriting. She quotes a lyric that's played in her mind. She finds that her smile comes easily.

He relaxes, says, come hang out on the bus with us, if you want.

She goes, because, why not? The night expands before her. She slides into a velour-covered seat and takes the beer that's passed to her. Nods when she's introduced, allows herself to be pulled in.

A velour-covered seat or a velour-covered sea. Later she'll write one, meaning the other. And then, in reading it, realize that the mistake is closer to the reality. There's the brief rush and lift of being off-course and suspended over time. Of being held aloft and separate from the ordinary and, so, from gravity.

The seat is a boat adrift upon a sea. For a time. For an extended moment.

Later she will write about the show, and then lose the thread of meaning and drift into another thought. She'll drink too much coffee to battle lack of sleep and to prolong the tingling otherworldliness. That sense of having jumped realities, lifted off from the ordinary into the extraordinary. Or perhaps just from one version of ordinary to another, but one so unfamiliar as to seem extraordinary, at least for the time being.

○

The art of letting go is not a rip, but an unknotting. A reversed cat's cradle. Each tangle undone feels like a return to breathing.

Bryn wakes in the morning, unsure of where she is at first. Her dreams flutter for a moment at the corners of the room, but before she can fully recall them, they're gone. The laptop lays twisted in the blankets. Bryn checks to see what she was working on when she drifted off, and then saves her work and closes the machine.

When she was a kid, she used to remember her dreams. They seemed to come in series with repeating themes. There were small anxieties reflected in the fabric of the dreams—tasks that couldn't be finished, houses with rooms that led into other rooms but never a door to the outside—but for the most part her childhood dreams were pastoral water colors tinted by the fairy tales and science fiction novels she devoured.

All dreams recede immediately upon waking. Sometimes a shadowy specter of a fleeting vision lasts just for a moment. But no longer. There's nothing but the haunting knowledge that it had come in the night.

○

Jude,

I heard from Andrea that you're working on something new. I'd like to hear it. Would you send me something?

Also, you're not so good at this keeping in touch thing. The way it works is I write to you and you respond.

It can also work if you write to me and I respond. Either of those.
Best,
B.

iii.

What Bryn thinks is that she needs to lose her heart again. Like a stiff muscle from over-exercising, the pain will only subside when the exercise is repeated. If she can push through her own awkwardness, the inner chill, the folding in of the self, the c-curve of the body around the solar plexus. If she can somehow expand beyond herself, beyond the shy exoskeleton that keeps her separate, then maybe. Just maybe.

Not that this is pain, really. And not that her heart is lost. There was just the one time crying in the car outside the club. Knowing Jude suddenly and irrevocably, and then continuing on as strangers on separate tracks. Trains passing.

Or is it ships?

But what if she doesn't want to be a solo captain? What if she wants to feel, again, the flush and unease of being close to someone. Turning a stranger into a friend. Risking the divide. Trading in perceived composure for the kinetic excitement of new conversations, new experiences.

Even as she thinks this, Bryn realizes how antiseptic she keeps her world. Tidy desk, tidy apartment. Deadlines never missed, bills never late. Conversations efficient, emotions in check. It took so long to achieve that unrockable equilibrium that now it's hard to be any other way. Still, Bryn wants to be rocked.

Or, at least consider being rocked.

The night hanging out on the tour bus was fun. Not wild, unbridled fun, but a warm memory only slightly tarnished by moments of uncertainty. Insecurity. Those flashes of having too many thumbs, knees and elbows that jab out in all the wrong directions. Too shrill of a laugh, an ache between the eyes from trying too hard to look friendly, interested, amused.

But no one else noticed, she tells herself. The only price to pay was the aura of a hangover and the sluggishness of too little sleep. Chug coffee, muscle through. Shake off the webbing and the down fill, try to remember a time when things were new and the edges were sharp. When rockstars were larger than life. When concerts were an adventure.

Sometimes Bryn wishes she had the music writer resume-worthy memory of a Ramones show. Anything at CBGB. Anything that might have left a battle scar. Her first real show, instead, could be one of a handful—The Red Hot Chili Peppers on a co-bill with Fishbone is the one she usually tells when someone asks.

What was your first show?

Like, *first* first? Or the first one that mattered? Or the first one that was worth telling other people about?

- The Paul Winter Consort.
- Steve Miller Band
- The Red Hot Chili Peppers (or, depending on who's asking, a punk band called False Prophets, or Odetta, or Jimmy Cliff)

When she was young, concerts just happened to her. That's how Bryn remembers it. She was in college before it occurred to her to go to the shows she wanted to go to. Up to that point, concerts and recorded music were unrelated. She bought the records she liked and went to the shows that were available and easy and free. It wasn't about *liking* the band as much as it was about being somewhere and doing something.

In the case of the False Prophets, she ended up in the backseat of their car for an hour while they drove around the city shooting footage with a battered camcorder. If she could do that as a teenager, why not now?

Now, when she had a reason. When she had an invitation. When the only thing missing was the leap of faith, the desire to cross the line from singular to part of something.

Her heart is not lost. Nor is it broken or wounded. Not even on her sleeve. Nothing. Stubbornly unmoved and locked in her rib cage, metaphors be damned.

The night on the bus was supposed to be a one-off, but it couldn't remain that. Bryn didn't even know why, exactly. Just that she was driven in that direction. Go out. Find something. Some connection. Something real and solid. Something beyond herself, her mind, the chatter of her brain.

Kind of like legitimizing a one-night stand. Going into it with the momentum, the blinders of alcohol and Friday (Saturday?), the longing for adventure, for different-ness, for escape.

Falling asleep, still twitchy with bravado and adrenaline, then waking a few short hours later, heart pumping. Fight or flight.

Is it fright or flight? Fright or fight?

The fright sits on the chest, beating its black wings. *Get up, fool. Outrun the memory of the night.*

Outrun it, or make an uneasy peace with it. Synthesize it. The dark shadows under the eyes, the purple bruise blooming on the neck. Own it. Say you want it like that. Say you meant to sleep there, wake up there. Say you're coming back. The next night, and the one after that.

Say it's what you want.

Say it until you believe it.

Bryn's nights, most of them, are not like that. Mostly she wakes early and alone, mind already crackling with the responsibilities of the day. She wonders, though, what if. What if she gives up a little bit of her correctness, her uprightness, her morning person-ness.

Not forever. Not even for a long time. Just for now. Just until she loses her heart. Her clean, correct, upright heart.

She begins the process of mining her inbox and her mailbox for the next thing. The band picture, the video, the single, the sound clip that makes her stomach drop or clench or whatever. The physical response.

The leaning in. The gasp. The breathless excitement.

Maybe not breathless, but something like it. The pulse quickening.

This is the place where, if the crush isn't yet a crush, the possibility of it is born. Where it's planted.

Then again, the way a crush works has little to do with willing a one night stand to turn into a legitimate relationship; it has little to do with finding a favorite new album in a stack of blind submissions. It's what happens in a moment, walking through town on a coffee break, taking in the scenery, the tourist crowds, the pigeons, the men playing chess in the park, the colors of the new dresses in the boutique windows.

And then there he is, rounding the corner. His bowler, his neckerchief, his missing incisor. His open smile. The question in his smile. The question that isn't a question.

✪

His name is Tobias Bridge. Rather, that's the name he goes by (borrowed from a seventeenth century English pirate) and, as such, has adopted a swashbuckling look. Black jeans tucked into tall boots, French-cuff shirts, or vests worn over a bare chest. A tattoo of an anchor on his bicep. That sort of thing. But somehow it isn't ironic. Somehow his stage persona comes off as genuine.

Bryn meets Tobias first and gets to know his music later. He walks into her life, the way strangers do. The way people do who are there in the background for weeks or months. Years, maybe. And then suddenly they emerge from the scenery. Their names and jobs and life details might not be known, but their presence is elevated to a level of importance. They're on the train, in the coffee shop, in line at the bank, buying organic lemons and steel-cut oats in the grocery store.

Tobias Bridge isn't buying lemons. But one day he's walking down the street with his band, wearing a top coat and carrying a paper bag from the record store. Bryn knows him instantly from his press photo: Tobias Bridge and the Buckaneers.

She says, hey, you're Tobias Bridge.

He looks pleased to be recognized. Poses for a photo. The first time, there's a girl with him. She steps into the frame and rests her pretty auburn head on his shoulder.

The next time there's no girl, just the guys in the band. They're a quartet—drummer, stand up bassist, keyboard player and Tobias singing and playing guitar. Bryn doesn't know this at first. She doesn't pursue the band. They're rootsy. They play jam festivals and summer festivals and Americana festivals. They have the sort of following that knows every word of Tobias' complicated songs.

Bryn comes to know all of this slowly, over years, over albums, over press releases and blog posts that come across her desk with increasing frequency.

Tobias Bridge isn't the sort of name you forget. And the bowler hat and the neckerchief—those details stick.

More so than organic lemons, more so than a stranger who becomes a familiar presence in the parking lot and the bank line.

○

The scariest place to see a show, for some reason, is the back stage of the record store downtown. It's the kind of place that would have felt right to Bryn when she was sixteen (if she had gone out much, if she'd been less timid) and now it feels like trying to go back to high school.

But why should it?

Does music have to have an age?

On the question of music vs. age:

1. Music is ageless

    a. Music keeps us young

    b. Music only becomes impossible to understand or relate to, or is only for the young when the listener stops trying

    c. But as the listener gets older and more experienced, and therefore possibly more biased, she has to try harder. Not just keep trying, but keep trying with greater resolve.

2. Musicians are not ageless

    a. Musicians who try to stay young (dyed hair, wearing the clothes they wore when they were young, cosmetic surgery) age faster than those who don't fight aging.

    b. Musicians who try to do what they've always done age faster than those who embrace change.

        i. Except for musicians who have always changed, like Bob Dylan

        ii. Or musicians who were never young, like Willie Nelson.

3. Blues musicians and Celtic musicians age better than rockstars, because their act is not dependent on youth.

4. There is some music that the aging music fan should just avoid. Or listen to only in secret. Hair metal, boy bands, etc.

5. Liking something *ironically* (or, at least perceived as ironically) allows one to like it for a bit longer.

6. Being genuinely interested trumps being cool or young or hip. Which is to say, if one is going to a show and doubts that one is the right age, don't then attempt to compensate with coolness or hipness. Just show up and be interested.

    a. And probably stand in the back.

    b. Or just go with it, and be the old person, and sit in the front, in the chair, if there's a chair to be had.

7. Finally, music is ageless, but even so, it doesn't always age well. Much of the Police repertoire has come through the decades with near-timeless grace. The same can not be said for Bobby Darin, or The Carpenters or Simple Minds. Which is not to say that they didn't perform great songs, it's just that those songs are of an era. An era that has passed.

Bryn goes to the show at the record store. She makes it her job, because it's easier with a notebook to hide behind. The stage is rough-hewn from plywood. There are a few battered couches and, along the side of the room, a couple of rows of movie theater seats. Bryn wedges herself into a corner, wishes she could drink a beer but the record store is a store and not a bar. The kids who've commandeered the couches have a case of beer cans at their feet. One of them, a boy with black nail polish and a studded dog collar, glances her way for a moment, sizes her up, then hands her a can.

She takes it. Toasts him.

Someone once told Bryn, to toast right you have to do two things: Make eye contact while you clink glasses, and then take a drink before you set your glass down. *You have to drink the luck you made with the toast*, was the explanation.

Bryn drinks the luck and stuffs in her ear plugs as the first peal of guitar rings into the room.

The show is good, but after it's over, there's no one to talk to. Just the kid (now drunk) on the couch. She says, thanks for the beer, and makes her way back into the street. Still herself. Still singular, an island in a sea of people.

Music is supposed to be the connective tissue. Bryn wonders why, for her, it's not. Not now. Not yet.

iv.

Who is the first musician who really made you listen, like really *listen?*

Ah, the game changer. Bryn thinks about it, even though she doesn't need to. The answer is never that far away. First day of school, first kiss, first international trip. First band that ever really reached you.

Violent Femmes, she says. And not just because of the song that says *fuck* like twenty times. But because of the weird instruments, the evocative lyrics. The dark humor. Maybe the fuck song was the gateway, but after the irreverence and angst, there was real art.

She still listens to them sometimes. Usually in the car, sometimes on a run. The kind of inbetween moments where it's okay to revisit the past without really reliving it. Glancing in the window, but not moving back into the house.

There were other bands before. Other musicians, other songs. When she was a little girl, she sang along to *Free To Be You And Me*. She liked the Kenny Loggins song that Kermit the Frog sang. Sometimes she danced to The Supremes, using a serving spoon as a microphone

But not until the Violent Femmes did she *need* the songs.

And then, when they released their fourth album, *3*, a weird thing happened. A guy at the college radio station, the station that Bryn called into with requests, gave her an extra copy of the demo tape. He said, make a tape of this tape, and then get rid of the demo.

Which didn't make sense because why *wouldn't* Bryn want the demo? It was the best thing ever. *Ever.*

But then everything went wrong. As soon as she put the demo into her backpack, bad things started to happen. She lost a library book, missed the bus. Just little things.

And then she failed a test and skinned her knee and it just got worse from there.

A girl, older and bigger, said she was going to kick Bryn's ass for talking to her boyfriend.

A boy Bryn barely knew. Gym class taunting. *Meet me in the parking lot after school.* Bryn walked home looking over her shoulder, shaken. She took the demo out of her bag at the record store, told the guy behind the counter that he could have it if he wanted it.

Cool, it's not even out yet, he said, holding up the cassette.

Don't keep it, said Bryn. It's cursed.

Cool, said the record store guy.

○

Tobias Bridge has a song about being cursed. Which was sort of funny because nothing about Tobias Bridge suggests a cursed man. Maybe the missing tooth, but he even manages to wear that with aplomb. He's off-kilter, listing slightly to one side or another but never toppling. He wears his hat askew and his hair (revealed only when his hat flies off, mid-performance) is hastily chopped and styled only by sweat and motion. His neckerchief is always in mid-flip, as is his easy grin. If he is, indeed, cursed, it's a curse that he accepts with the grudging pride one might have for a scar from a knife fight.

Bryn thinks about this, but not at first. It's not the song about the curse that sticks with her. It's a different song—a silly one about a fairy-tale princess. It's all kick drum and accordion and shouted lyrics. The kind of thing that buskers play on the street on warm summer evenings. The sort of thing you can listen to a hundred times without ever letting the lyrics touch you.

> *You think you're an outsider, baby, that's just fine*
> *I'm an outcast, too. You're one of my kind.*

Bryn doesn't hear the sliver of a verse so much as feel the brute force of it. Not that Tobias even knows her, or anything about her, but that line was written for her. After that, she can hear him. His voice: the ragged edge of it, the way he's ruined it over the years for the sake of his music. The more ruined his voice gets, the better his songs are. The tatters and raw edges carry the emotion. But he can still hit a high note with all of the soft and sad sincerity of a jilted lover.

Once she can hear him, Bryn starts to look for him. She looks, first, in her record collection and in her backlog of articles, and finds him in both places. He's been with her for years. On the roster of showcase bands, as an opener for bigger acts she wrote about. She interviewed him once when he wrote a handful of songs for the soundtrack of an independent film; she's written his name a dozen times or more.

And after all of this time, he suddenly arrives. Tobias with his hats and his vintage coats. Tobias with his alias which took over his life years ago, absorbing the person he once was, but could no longer be in the hungry wake of his stage persona. Tobias, a smallish man, but a presence large enough to take up space in the small world of Bryn Thompson. A vision large enough to capture the imagination of a music writer whose imagination was well-versed in running wild. A voice large enough to crack the quiet.

○

It's much less intimidating to go to a big club. Especially armed with an iPad. It can be pretty much any kind of show—the sort where middle-age couples come out and sip beers while sitting at the tables in the back; the sort where teenagers in spiky haircuts press up against the pit—the can between the crowd and the stage where the photographers lurk. The setting is familiar. Bryn knows what to do, how to act, where to stand. The trick is to hover at the end of the bar, or behind the speakers at the side of the stage.

On the other hand, trying to work during a sold out show is its own particular kind of torture. Standing in a crowd while holding an iPad, it's impossible to blend in.

What are you doing, reading an ebook?

Are you some kind of writer or something?

Bryn says, yes. You know how you read reviews of shows online? How do you think they get there?

If there's a glamorous part to her job, standing in a crowded club typing into an iPad in the dark is not it.

Bryn packs up her iPad and starts to head home, but on the way out she passes by the merch table and something tells her to stop. She's tried this before—the night on the bus—and it didn't end badly. So what, she thinks. What could go wrong?

This is the connecting with people experiment.

She could say, hey, I loved your set. She could say that and then leave.

She could say, hey, I'm a music writer—I'd love to interview your band.

She could say, do you all want to get a drink?

Bryn could say any of that. But she's not sure which way to go. She's frozen in uncertainty.

✪

The first time she has a conversation with Tobias is in a bar on New Year's Eve. There's a concert in the auditorium around the corner, one of those all-night shows with bands stacked in layers, and then jam-sessions between sets. It's not midnight yet, but people on the street are already drunk.

The bar is a sanctuary of sorts. A Spanish place. A place masquerading as Spanish, with a tapas menu and tiled countertops and romantic alcoves painted in cozy, earthy tones. Couples are eating late meals and sharing bottles of wine. Their faces are warmed by candlelight and expensive clothing. Bryn plants herself on a stool, orders a drink, waits for her friends to arrive.

She's not out with a guy. Maybe she should be. The loveliness of the atmosphere makes her wonder why she's not, why she's just tagging along on a group New Year's Eve outing. She halfway hopes her friends won't show and she'll have the night to herself, to be lonely alone, rather than in a group of people who are alone together and trying desperately to hide from loneliness.

And then Tobias is there, in a velvet blazer and silk scarf. Shined shoes. She sees the glint of the shoes, first, out of the corner of her eye. Then feels the soft brush of his sleeve against her bare arm as he reaches for the menu.

She wants to say, hey, I know you. (Only she doesn't know him)

She wants to say, remember when I took your picture back in the fall?

She doesn't say, I love your music (though she does) or, your last album was your most fully-realized (though it was, and she saved those songs in a special playlist, a playlist for the songs that tell her something about *herself*) or, how do you maintain your energy for the duration of a show?

Instead she says, hello.

He smiles a sideways smile. Generous mouth, eyes hidden in the shadow of his hat brim. He says, I don't know what I want to drink.

She says, go for the Granache. It's good. She points to it on his menu, the inexpensive one at the top. Says again, it's good. Cheap, but surprisingly nice.

126

He says, okay. Leans forward, orders it from the bartender. Two glasses. Then turns and hands one to the girl who's been waiting behind him. She's all suede-boots-long-hair-lace-hem-Bohemian. *Of course she is.*

Tobias is quickly absorbed by the crowd. His absence is a resounding echo.

Bryn looks for him after that. Sort of. She goes where her group goes, bouncing from bar to bar and into the streets at midnight for the fireworks. It would be nice to see Tobias Bridge, but what would she do?

New Year's kisses are for the people with whom you intend to spend the year. *Begin as you mean to continue.* Who would be foolish enough to kiss a rockstar?

☼

Bryn steps into a dim low-ceilinged bar-turned-listening room where she's meeting the filmmaker Leo Barry. It's a new project—a documentary about touring bands—and Leo asked her to help with a few of the interviews. This one is Brave Ulysses.

The camera crew sets up in the gloom while the bartender takes chairs down from tables where they were set for sweeping. The bar smells of stale beer, but it also smells of cedar paneling and, pleasantly, of age.

Eventually a van pulling a trailer rolls up and five guys in crumpled flannels and scuffed boots pile out. They shake hands with Leo, they high-five the bartender. They amble back to the van where a road crew of two has started unloading a small mountain of gear.

Bryn makes herself useful carrying boxes of t-shirts to the merch booth. She makes small talk, she sits on a barstool while the guitarist, Jake, changes his strings. She listens while he talks about a fight he's having with his wife in bits and pieces, across state lines and over days and weeks.

It's hard, he says. There's a fine web of lines around his eyes. Premature crow's feet from sleepless nights, bad food, stress.

At night, when the crowd is thick and the drinks are flowing, the bar feels like a rec room. A humid womb. A world apart from the world. An inner sanctum.

In the late-afternoon daylight, empty but for road-weary musicians and roadies, it's more of a shell. There's a sad pall that surprises Bryn.

It's a part of the life of the touring musician that she rarely sees. She knows about the stage. She knows what they say in interviews. She knows what to ask, how to get them to open up about their creative processes, their aspirations, even their disappointments. But how do you ask about the in between times? The grinding miles, the ache of sleep deprivation, the people on the other end of a dropped phone call.

How do you like L.A.? Bryn asks.

Jake shrugs. I hate it. That's off the record. L.A. has been good to us, but I don't like it. I hate the driving and how far everything is. I'm sick of the scene. I'm just…he trails off.

Bryn says, tell me where you'd like to live.

He's quiet for a moment. We're thinking about Nashville, he says. That's off the record, too. And I don't care about living in Nashville, but when I can't sleep at night I think about getting a farmhouse in the country-side, maybe even a horse or something. Maybe a tractor.

A tractor?

Jake laughs. Crazy, right? I'm not going to be a farmer or anything, but my grandpa had a tractor, when I was a kid, and he used to take me for rides. It's where I go in my mind, you know?

She does know. She has her places, too. Places she can go in the dark of night and when her confidence flags and when her heart feels heavy. Places she can go when the noise is too loud and not pleasant, when the silence is unreachable. Or when the silence is oppressive and inescapable.

Bryn goes to the turquoise water of the Caribbean, floating on her back in the bathtub warmth, the blue sky above, her body weightless. Or that's where she did go. Now she goes to the room where Jude Archer waits to answer her questions.

Where Jude Archer paints a bodiless head with stars in its hair.

Where Jude Archer practices surrendering to his art, to god, to the universe, to whatever.

But Bryn isn't thinking of him at the moment. She keeps her focus on Jake, on his story and the clues he reveals.

Later, after sound check, Leo films the band in the green room while Bryn nudges them along with questions.

Pete, what kinds of bands were you in before you all started Brave Ulysses?

Seth, do you remember imagining going on tour before you actually did it for the first time? What's the major difference between what you imagined it would be like and what it's actually like?

Jake, what has L.A. given your music that no other place could give you?

They loosen up as the interview goes on, their faces relaxing, their postures opening. They joke and rib each other like brothers. They get on each other's nerves and calm each other with easy touches.

What did you give up to pursue this dream? Bryn asks. There's a chink in the armor then. She's asked the question before. It's one she pulls out from time to time because it's a question that interests her. What does anyone give up to achieve a goal?

The weariness returns to Jake's face.

Later, Leo will show her stills from the shoot. The guys in the band caught in various moments of focus and distraction. There's Jake, his guitar propped up on the bar as he changes a string. He leans into a beam of light, his eyes haunted as he glances up.

That's intense, Bryn says. She tucks the c-curl of hair back behind her ear.

I don't know what you said to him, but you really got something, Leo says.

I didn't say anything special.

Maybe you could come along and not say anything special to the next band I'm shooting? Leo says.

Bryn nods.

Leo says, seriously. You got some good material from those guys.

What he doesn't ask is, *What's the secret?*

What Bryn doesn't answer is, *There's no secret.*

V.

Bryn thinks that maybe she should stop being herself. Just for awhile. Maybe if she pretends, with enough conviction, to be someone else, she'll be able to cross over. But who to be?

There's a conflicting push-pull to be completely genuine and to be completely contrived. The genuine self is so raw, so open to the elements and to the hypochondriasis brought on by living completely exposed. The genuine self seeks, always, to balm its wounds and buffer its tender heart.

The contrived self, however, is a facade. A plexiglass wall, an armor of Novocaine. The contrived self can be battered, cut open, left to scab and heal, twisted and rugged but stronger than before. It's a surrogate, a sounding board.

Bryn sees her double in her mind, a girl of her same size and features, but with more confidence, more polish, more of a glinting edge. The second Bryn knows what the first one knows and thinks and wants, but she knows and thinks and wants through a filter of ballerina poise and Mad Max tough. She carries herself as if she's in a leather jumpsuit at all times. She moves through life with the stealth and assuredness of a super-spy, eyes at the back of her head, throwing star and pearl-handled pistol at the ready.

The second Bryn would not shy away from talking to strangers or to bands. She would demand backstage passes, she would make out with boys.

Maybe with girls. Whatever.

She'd try things, go places, miss work, blow by deadlines and boundaries.

Is that right? Is that accurate?

The first Bryn isn't sure. Her alter ego has already gone too far. Too much badness, too much nonchalance.

The contrived self can be an enhanced version of the genuine self, but it can't be wholly other. It has to be based in the same reality, cut from the same cloth.

My stage persona is just a cooler version of me, says Tobias Bridge. *Louder, crazier, able to do things that I might not be able to do if I was just being myself.*

Only, of course, the contrived self is carried through the world in the vessel of the genuine self. The two feel separate and yet are never apart.

The two feel the same and yet one is cleaved from the other. A pair of twins made with a deft slice. They share a face, a mind, a brilliant red slash of parting. They will revel in their separation and then they will spend forever trying to knit themselves back together again.

Like a sleep walker, the contrived self parts the crowd, strides to the stage, the merch booth, the VIP box. She's at home on tall heels, at home with a whiskey in her hand, at home with a throaty laugh and a one night stand and the kind of hair that, in the morning, looks like she was handled roughly.

The genuine Bryn has no stomach for rough treatment. Not for harsh words or bruises or tangled hair.

But maybe if she had a leather jumpsuit, a throwing star, a pearl-handled pistol…Maybe if she could drink enough to forget the wall between the two selves: The armed border crossing between who she knows how to be and who she doesn't dare to be.

Isn't sure how to be.

Can't remember how to be.

Sometimes dreams of being.

Sometimes, says Tobias Bridge, *I think only my mom knows me as I once was, and only because she's kept all the photo albums. Only she calls me by the name I was born with, and that's probably because she gave me that name.* He pauses for a moment, the name resting on his tongue, but he doesn't say it. He's fully enmeshed in the being of Tobias Bridge.

Because, he says, *even I forget where one of us ends and the other begins.*

○

The funny thing about Niall Davies is that he's exactly the way his songs suggest he'd be. Soft spoken, sleepy, almost fading into the shadows of the listening room. Bryn meets him there during soundcheck. He seems lost, drifting from the spotlight to the door where they shake hands. Bryn has a short list of questions for him; they're speaking on video—a new one in Leo Barry's series—about Niall's tour and his album. It's the third in a triptych that's taken him a decade to complete.

There's something about the awkwardness of the interview that puts Bryn at ease. Niall mumbles and whispers his way through each answer. But, if he's given enough time, at the end of each statement he says something witty and barbed. Something incredibly sharp for a guy who passes himself off as a stoned British surfer.

That, and he talks with a strange sort of formality. It's probably the accent, Bryn thinks. He's wearing a cowboy hat and ratty Converse low-tops. His beard looks like a wild animal on his face. But then he offers to get her a drink from the bar, wants to know what the town is like, thanks her for taking the time.

He says, I think I was here before. Two years ago, maybe. I think I played some sort of hippy cafe. He says it like *CAFfay*.

Do you remember seeing me here before? he asks.

Not at a hippy cafe, says Bryn.

Then maybe it was somewhere else, says Niall. Or maybe it'll happen in the future.

If that's the case, I'll look forward to it, Bryn tells him.

Later, after the show, Bryn goes to the side of the stage to talk to Niall. Just to say something encouraging. *Good to see you*, or *good show*, or *the audience loved it* or whatever. But he's already talking to someone.

The tall woman who danced in front of the stage the whole time. Even though it wasn't really dancing music. Even though it was more of a contemplative show, the sort where one sips a cocktail and thinks about the fleetingness of life.

The tall woman doesn't look like someone who bothers much with the fleetingness of life. From a distance she could be twenty-five. Sun-bronzed and blond, her hair a cascade around her tan cheekbones. She wears a braided headband and a peasant top that dips off one tan shoulder, and bootcut jeans that cling to her hips. Her wrists jangle with silver and turquoise bracelets when she lifts a manicured hand to touch Niall's face.

It's an intimate gesture. Bryn waits for Niall to look bothered, annoyed, violated. Instead, he looks relaxed. Flattered. Maybe he's into this woman. Or at least into the attention.

Maybe that's how it goes.

Probably.

But as Bryn's about to back away, the woman catches her eye. Looks bothered and annoyed. Wraps a territorial arm around Niall's waist and

133

purrs, I'll let you meet and greet.

She's actually older. A well preserved forty-five. Fit, lean, expensive but eager. And then she drifted away in a cloud of amber musk.

I was only saying good night, Bryn says.

She can't do what the amber musk woman was doing. She can't push her way into Niall's space, nor does she want to. She doesn't feel that way, doesn't feel the pull. To his music, yes. But not to him as a person.

And now she's chased off his groupie.

I'm sorry about...Bryn waves vaguely in the direction of the fading amber musk.

No worries, says Niall. I'll see her later.

Which is how it goes.

Of course it is.

☉

Sometimes it's hard for Bryn to begin new, with the next story. Sometimes it's exciting—the promise of the next adventure. The next big thing. But often it's at least a little bit sad.

To begin again means to move away from the last project. The last story. The last musician whose story was threaded, even if only for a few days, into Bryn's own story. And then that thread comes to an abrupt end and there's a new thread, ready for the fabricating.

Sometimes, to begin, Bryn has to nurse the wound of what's past. Go back and listen to the songs from before. The songs that took on meaning and importance.

Sometimes she has to sleep with the lights on. A light from another room cutting a passage through the dark.

The old songs are a light into the new story. Sometimes. Not always.

Sometimes the way in is simple. A quote that jumps out from a press release. A piquant verse in a song.

1. I read that you recorded this album all over New Orleans; that you recorded the drums in a French Quarter shotgun shack and one guitar in a lake house. Did the instruments determine the places or vice versa?

2. If you had a mobile recording studio, what cities or towns or neighborhoods would be on your list to record in?

3. Which do you prefer to make, an LP or an EP?

She's heard that it can be hard for the musicians who tour from town to town each night, meeting people briefly and intensely, and then moving on. They've told her, some of them, of this peculiar heartbreak. A side effect of the job.

Bryn wonders if she doesn't suffer from the same affliction, only she's the one who's left, over and over. Always left behind. Just the voice on the phone, a disembodied presence too easily disconnected.

Sid Holmes, who's been doing this for more than thirty years, tells Bryn that relationships on the road happen quickly. Sped up, in contrast to the way time slows down in between stops, when it's just miles on the highway stretching out toward an unreachable horizon.

He says, it's always a pleasure to get to spend some time, each night, with the people who've spent time getting to know my music and lyrics. It always seems like they know me so much better than I can ever know them, but I do my best after the show to even that up.

Bryn wonders how. How can Sid Holmes open himself up to a roomful of strangers each night? There's no time for the usual detective work, the clues that divide strangers into groups: Potential friends and people who could never be your friends.

Maybe he doesn't discern. There's no time for discernment, only time to be open, to let it all in. The rest of the night, alone in a hotel room and the following day, alone in a car, heading to the next town—that's the time for putting the guard back up.

But who needs their guard up when they're all alone?

So, maybe Sid Holmes lives without the guard up.

Bryn can't do that. Not yet. Not now. She listens to the next band through the muffled wall of her own invisible protection. She listens without allowing anything in. If any sound or word or nuance can breach her armaments, then she knows this is something special.

Then again, it's all something special. Even that which is unrealized and unperfected has its moments of genius. Find those, turn the key. Move forward and love again.

Not love. Wrong word.

Be interested, amused, curious. Find the way in. The light from another room.

○

Tobias Bridge is on the other side of the country wondering what thrift shop he should visit. He posts a photo of the band standing at the edge of the Grand Canyon, he posts a photo of himself playing foosball with a Hells Angel. He posts a photo of himself with a week's worth of beard. He posts a picture of the band's van, broken down outside of Lake Tahoe or Reno or Boise. Someplace. He's everywhere and nowhere. His life is a roadmap of photographs and quick bursts of information. He calls his fans beautiful freaks. He buys new boots, he wears big rings, he longs for a home-cooked meal and when he says this, some kind-hearted woman takes him home and feeds him in her kitchen.

Bryn watches the progress of Tobias unfold. It's not progress so much as a random dotting of the map. Tradewinds, jet streams, time zones, blue highways. She catalogues his moves with detached interest, an anthropologist studying the migratory patterns of a not-so-rare bird: The rockstar.

Tobias is often less rockstar, more gypsy.

Dapper vagabond, erudite hobo, post-modern raconteur.

iv.

The next band is fronted by two brothers. This is an old story. Bryn's immediately pulled in. She likes brothers. Wishes she had a brother. She likes the wholesome air of family bands, even if they're not wholesome. There's still something there. Some kernel of loyalty, history, blood being thicker.

Thick bloodedness.

Bryn likes how siblings in a band can't help but, at turns, stand up for each other and then tear each other down. They defend too fiercely and one-up too quickly. They smirk, punch, behave badly. They're too good at pushing each other's buttons. But they also have an innate sense of each other's timing, rhythm and harmony.

Nothing makes Bryn more homesick for a past that was never hers than to be in the presence of brother musicians.

This new band reminds her, in a way, of every other family band she's interviewed. But especially the Silvers brothers who were her pet project for a time. They were unknowns, but good at social media and good looking. Wholesome but handsome. Raised in a church but able to shimmy into tight jeans and the slinkiest guitar solos. They'd grown up unaware of U2, The Cure, Bruce Springsteen or The Clash and then, when they hit college and were turned loose in the world, they found it all and ingested it the way most college kids ingest beer and pizza. Total immersion. Total synthesis. They emerged, four years later, with Bachelor's degrees and a catalog of contagious mid-tempo rockers that immediately charmed anyone who the Silvers brothers could convince to listen.

Bryn championed them. Their first EP, their sexy (if naive) swagger, their bleachy smiles. Their shows attracted mostly girls, at first, except both of the Silvers boys could turn out a searing guitar solo and pull off a backflip from the stage.

And then, just when it looked like they'd lined up their local fan base and were on their way to something bigger—national radio play, a label deal, their song placed in the closing credits of the sort of movie that people actually mentioned when speaking of great movie sound tracks—they moved to Germany. To record a next album, they said. To really get away from the distractions and focus on songwriting.

They were never heard from again.

This new band of brothers (there are three, this time) has just as much promise. They present a unified front, wearing pressed suits on stage, setting their shows with antique lamps and designing sepia-toned posters. They seem solid, but if Bryn was a fortune teller, she'd say they had three good years. Maybe another year or two of falling apart. One brother will get married and have a kid. One will realize he likes designing posters more than going on tour. The third will start his own project and maybe he'll make it as a solo act.

Maybe he'll wither without his brothers, noisy and chaotic, crowded around him.

Or maybe Bryn is wrong. She's not a fortune teller. She can't predict the future.

☼

The decision to write about Tobias Bridge is not a hard one. It's almost not a decision at all. When the assignment is handed down, Bryn feels like she's already been doing research for years. This musician who was once a stranger is now a familiar presence, skirting her life. They have a history, albeit a loosely-strung one.

To listen to his songs for a week or so is no chore. Most of them are familiar anyway. To watch him sing on video brings him closer, his boyish face contorted with the effort of pushing out the words. He doesn't sing so much as do battle. His guitar has taken a beating. Sometimes he punishes a tambourine or a floor tom just to get his point across.

Bryn is pleasantly surprised that she likes the songs. Even if they're folky. And often sad. She likes the insistence, the energy, the tsunami of raw intensity that knocks her back. Tobias gave up on gentle folk at some point—or maybe that was never his thing—and took up the cross of full-assault folk rock. He tells stories. He hurls stories. He bludgeons his listeners with words and images, with his bloodied heart, with his bruised fists. And then he grins his sweet boyish grin, wipes the sweat from his brow, looks like he wants to pull everyone in for a group hug.

The questions come easily, too:

Some of your songs feel like fist-pumping battle cries. Was the intention to incite something within your listeners? And if you could incite some emotion, what would it be?

You tour so much that you have tours between your tours. Do you ever want to just be still?

Can you write songs when you're on the road?

Can you write songs when you're not on the road?

You sing so hard—do you ever injure your voice?

I read about an Indian saint who hugs everyone who comes to her for darshan. She's hugged so many people that she can no longer move her arms without help. Are you losing your voice like that?

Are you giving your voice for our sins?

The questions come easily, but what's harder is the permission. The permission to follow the thread, to know Tobias Bridge in her mind. Not just intellectually, not just with the parts of her mind that love questions, but with the parts of her mind that love stories, love travel, love adventure, love a character, love a certain vocal quality, a certain instrumentation, a certain poetry.

The part of her mind that loves love.

Is it weird to feel like one is cheating by loving a new thing when one has already pledged oneself to a different thing?

It's human to love more than one thing. Probably more than one person. And to confuse things with people is even more human.

It's human to say that there's more than one type of love, but it's hard to believe that. Romantic love floats to the top every time, even though humans go through the day professing their love for everything else—ice cream, shoes, vocations, movies, songs, album art, Dachshund puppies.

People don't feel guilty about loving Dachshunds or fro-yo as much as (if not more than) their kids or spouses.

Because there are different sorts of love.

Puppy love is always acceptable because who can resist a puppy?

But Tobias Bridge is no puppy.

○

What Bryn thinks is that she needs to lose her heart again. But standing on the precipice, one giant leap from losing, she's not so sure. Losing always hurts, doesn't it? She hasn't thought it through. And all those times

141

seeing Tobias Bridge in passing, him just a colorful flash in the background, she hadn't realized he was making his imprint.

Or was he?

Because that's what she thought, too, with Jude Archer. That he was marking her. Through his songs, through his art, through his world vision, through the tide of his being that gathered her up and swept her along.

But what if she was the tide, the touch, the incriminating finger print. What if she was the one choosing. Who to reach out to. Who to care about. Whose words to make known. Whose songs to commit to memory, whose voice to cherish, who to pull in to intimate conversation. Whose voice to press to her ear, whose heart to claim, to carry.

And then, maybe, to lay down again.

○

His hands are in her hair, his fingers pressing against her scalp, lifting the weight of her hair away from her head. Fingers long and thin, drawing subtle lines over her head. Crop circles. Demarcations.

Incantations.

She could lose herself in this, even as he's saying, you shouldn't put your hair in a ponytail so often. Those rubber bands break your hair.

I don't use rubber bands, Bryn says. She's picturing the fleshy office supply kind.

He holds up the black elastic that she arrived with. The sin. Her sin.

No ponytails and less shampoo he says. His hands are still in her hair, separating the strands. Lifting it and examining it.

Bryn doesn't want much. Just for her hair to be made nice again. The split ends scissored off, a wash and blowdry. Hair care is a hassle, but a necessary one. Bryn knows she goes too long between appointments. She lets her color dull, she relies on her trusty ponytail. There's nothing this stylist can say to change her, but she's willing to listen and murmur encouragingly as long as he keeps touching her head.

Going to the salon was a snap decision. She saw the guy, Andy, walking down the street with his long hair swaying from beneath his fedora. He's all long, skinny legs and skinny jeans and the bouncy, loose-jointedness that comes from being in one's twenties.

She knew she wanted to be around him for a few minutes.

She knew he cut hair.

She knew she was overdue for a trim.

With her head tilted back in the sink, her neck exposed and her eyes fixed on the ceiling, she's helpless. Almost helpless. Willing to be helpless. She lets herself be rocked and swayed. Warm water, fruity shampoo. Strong fingers rubbing her scalp and then massaging her neck. She could stay here forever, eyes closed, lost.

That's not true. Part of Bryn—a large part with a loud voice—can't stand the closeness. Wants to leap up, head in a halo of soap bubbles, and flee the salon.

A part of Bryn—a part with a strong grip—can't stand the thought of making a scene. And so she stays, relaxing and then tensing.

In front of the mirror, her body buried under the black cape, she watches her own face emerge through the scissors and the comb. She becomes herself again, a self who looks familiar but hard to place. The face in the mirror. The self everyone else sees. So why is Bryn so far removed from this face she wears every day?

The guy, Andy, looks like his clothes should reek of cigarette smoke and last night's drunk. Instead, he smells of pine and citrus. Clean and woodsy. His voice is rich and low. He speaks conspiratorially, like it's just them against the world. Bryn likes this. Likes being an insider. Likes being pulled into this guy's world, even as she's looking forward to being away from him and his touch and his knowingness.

She's thinking all of this and so, at first, his words don't break through her inner monologue.

He says, you write about music don't you?

She says yes. She knows where this is going. She doesn't want it to go there.

I have a band, he says. Maybe you can hear us play sometime.

Bryn wonders if anyone ever sees her. The her of the mirror, the her in her mind, the her who walks to work and eats a sandwich for lunch and wears a ponytail even though she shouldn't.

To the guy, Andy, she says, yeah. Okay, sometime. She's already leaving him, already walking out the door.

Part five

The interview with Tobias Bridge isn't going to be the usual interview, but a video interview with Leo Barry. They'll meet the band after soundcheck, record a song and five minutes of questions. It'll all be edited together for a package that will run on *Mic Stand's* web site. Bryn feels the adrenaline kick, and then the sinking feeling of self-doubt.

She might have a decade and a half under her belt as an interviewer, but not on video. Even with freshly cut hair. Even with the right clothes, with the right lighting, with all of the elements falling into place, it's her questions that matter.

And what if they're not right? On video, there're no go-to questions. No back up questions. No hedging, no negotiating.

Of course there are retakes and edits, but still, every question counts.

Even with that knowledge—with the fear that prickles when she tries to imagine the interview—the truth is that Bryn isn't as scared going into the video with Tobias Bridge as she was about meeting Jude Archer at soundcheck.

Either:
1. She's changed and is more sure of herself, or
2. She's changed and doesn't care as much, or
3. She hasn't changed but doesn't care about Tobias, or
4. There is some newfound certainty to this particular project that has never existed before.

Bryn read somewhere that fear is good because it keeps one safe. It keeps rock climbers from making rash moves. It reminds skydivers to open their chutes. But it doesn't keep them from climbing rocks or jumping out of planes in the first place, so how dependable is fear, anyway?

She feels afraid when she writes a question on a scrap of paper. Then she reads it back to herself and it sounds good. She reads it out loud, doesn't cringe at the sound of her own voice.

She's not fearless, but she's not frozen in the headlights of the oncoming tractor trailer, either.

Tobias is an oncoming tractor trailer. A train racing toward a mountain pass. A destiny of a sort.

Bryn doesn't know if she believes in destiny. It sounds suspicious— unprovable and shrouded in the mists of faith and superstition. But still. She'd like something to believe in. A talisman, a touchstone. A fate awaiting her eventual arrival.

A destiny with an askew bowler hat and a missing incisor.

○

The road to the club, the gold wash of late afternoon sun, the swept wooden floors, the scent of fresh air mixing with spilled beer, sweat and regret.

Here we go again.

Regret tinged with excitement, because regret is only regret when we don't learn the lesson and take the same wrong turn over and over. The swerve that leads to the pounding skull, the cracked rib, the busted lip. Or worse. Some wound not bad enough to leave a mark. And so the memory fades quickly and the swerve is still there waiting.

The bar, late in the afternoon, looks innocuous and feels like time stopped. The crunch of gravel under tires, the shouts of the guys from the kitchen setting up. The bartenders muscling kegs in through the side door. The alley stacked with broken down boxes and tall garbage cans full of empty bottles. There's a courtyard overgrown with tangled vines and scattered with brown leaves, but it hints at something magical come evening.

Or not magical. Just clusters of smokers listening to the band through the open door.

And there's a band on stage, sound checking. Tobias Bridge at the mic. He tests his vocal. Hoarse already. How he likes it.

This is where the swerve has taken him. Into so many bars, so many green rooms, so many alleys stacked with boxes and so many road miles slicing through dark. Ruining his voice to wrench out another drop of feeling. Tattooing his memories on his arm, writing his life down in songs. Taking the next swerve for the next song. Taking the kick, the punch, standing back up and spitting out a tooth.

146

Tobias Bridge looks through the gloom, spots Bryn watching from the doorway and says, just one more minute and I'm all yours.

He doesn't know that this makes her feel strange. That she flushes and goes to the restroom to blot her shiny forehead and fix her lipstick. *Ten deep breaths. Maybe five will do the trick. Should've had a beer first. Should go to the bar and order a shot.*

She's going to do just that, except when she walks out of the bathroom, Leo is there setting up his camera. Wants to know where she'd like to do the shoot.

Maybe in the courtyard? The light is nice.

And while they're setting up equipment the band is filing out, making introductions, shaking hands. Lugging the stand up bass out to the brick walkway. Kicking discarded cigarette butts out of the way.

Tobias is spraying his throat with a homeopathic concoction. He doesn't wink, but his face contains a wink hidden in its shadows.

Rules for making a video:

1. Sit closer to the subject than seems reasonable or feels comfortable. Spaces on video look larger than they do in real life. Sit close enough to touch, and then don't touch. Just a sliver of light between two bodies.

2. Interview the least amount of people. Interviewing a full band on camera is a train wreck, unless it's for a full-length documentary. Interview only one person if possible and no more than two.

3. Ask the questions once, off camera, so the subject has time to think about the answers.

4. Ask the questions twice, on camera, because the second round of responses will always be more concise and therefore better.

    a. That said, the first round of questions will feel better and more natural.

    b. Video is an exercise in going against natural.

5. For the interviewer: Blot first. Blot often. If in doubt, blot.

6. And don't fidget. Don't squint, scratch, pull faces, show teeth, laugh too much or touch your face. (See 4 b.)

The band plays first: the title track from their new album. The one Bryn calls anthemic (to herself). She says that word out loud and immediately questions her pronunciation. ANthemic? AnTHEME-ic?

They play the song again, stomping, picking up steam. Beating a tambourine, howling through the chorus. Bryn dances off camera. Not dances so much as bounces on her toes. She dances in her mind and it telegraphs through her legs.

And then it's time for the interview. The band files back into the club. The courtyard is pre-dusk. Twinkling lights strung along dried grapevines come on. Leo turns the camera toward a wrought iron bench and matching table. Bryn sits down, glad her black jeans and Converse sneakers are hidden behind the furniture.

Glad she braided her hair instead of the usual ponytail.

Hopes there's no lipstick on her teeth.

Tobias slides in next to her. Close. Close enough for video. Close enough to see the pattern on his neckerchief. His jacket is dark denim. Deadstock, probably. Something from the '60s forgotten in a faded, dusty Midwestern mercantile and then discovered by Tobias on a day off from tour.

His jeans are tucked into well-oiled boots. They are the only thing he's wearing that's nice. Even the leather cuff at his wrist is battered, though it looks like something marking a memory. A place or person he wanted to take with him.

Anytime you're ready, says Leo. The camera rolls.

Bryn smiles her video smile. Begins: your songs seem autobiographical. When you're having an experience, do you ever find yourself thinking, this will make a great song?

And then Tobias does the most extraordinary thing. Looks her in the eye. Puts his elbows on the table and leans toward her, like he's really listening, really interested. Like he's making a toast and drinking the luck. Like there's just the two of them and this moment and this courtyard and the rest of the world could end right then and he wouldn't give a damn.

She dreams that her nail-polish is not just chipped but worn away. Ground away. Chipped and scraped and scratched off until only a grimy crust of color remains.

She dreams that an old man is sitting in a chair in the corner of the room watching her sleep. She thinks, oh it's okay, it's just my grandfather.

And then her lucid mind remembers that she never met her grandfather. He has been dead longer than she has been alive. Her sleeping mind grapples with this injection of reality. Holds it up to the murky light of the dream world, turns it around and around, examines it from all sides and decides to discard it.

The old man sits there, unmoved. He doesn't need the sleeping mind to know him.

She dreams that she's late for work, but she can't seem to get all of her things packed into her bag. Keys, phone, lipstick, glasses, a book to read, perhaps some aspirin, a sample-sized vial of perfume…She wants to smell the perfume but she can't. Her sleeping mind describes it for her, but she doesn't believe. God or perfume, she has to experience it for herself.

She dreams that she's tangled in the sheets. She dreams that her hair has grown during the night and threatens to strangle her. She dreams that she's bound and thrown in the water, but even as her restrained body sinks, she feels none of the fear that she expects to feel. Instead, she finds that her body can adapt, can undulate like a fish, even with her arms pinned at her side. She moves in an easy rhythm through the water.

The thought crosses her mind that she'll soon run out of air, and so she takes the tiniest sip of breath under water. She's not surprised to find that she can breathe. Of course she can. She was made to live on land or in the sea. She has always known this.

❂

Tobias Bridge is like a foggy truth that Bryn has long suspected. *He does the most extraordinary thing. Looks her in the eye. Puts his elbows on the table and leans toward her, like he's really listening, really interested. Like there's just the two of them and this moment and this courtyard and the rest of the world could end right then and he wouldn't give a damn.* This is the simplest gesture, but also the most complex.

Everything stops and is reset and begins again at this point. The hallway that they were walking down a few minutes ago, that one that was just an ordinary hallway (interview, shake hands, walk away) is now a corridor of doors. Every door is a possibility.

1. Interview, shake hands, walk away.
2. Stay here in this spot and say everything that has to be said.
3. Reconvene later and see what comes of it.

Every door is its own lifetime, though there is no rule that once one door is entered, no other door can ever be entered. A person can open any or all of the doors. Just to look in, or to walk through and come back, or to walk through and never return. Choose your own adventure.

✲

Door 1.

In the afternoon light, there's a glint in Tobias' eye. It flickers and then stills. He answers each question easily, openly. He has nothing to hide. He is storied. Not an open book, but a book. Neither open nor closed. Everything is there, within the pages, waiting to be read.

Leo turns off the camera, gives a nod. The nod that means everything went well. They don't have to do a second take. But Bryn would stay there all evening doing take after take. She doesn't want to move, doesn't want to leave the moment.

Even as she's thinking that she doesn't want to move, she's already in motion. Standing, smoothing her jeans with her palms. Tobias is shaking Leo's hand, saying thanks for the opportunity.

That's what people say. Nice to meet you. Have a good day. Take care. Thanks for the opportunity.

Tobias says, that was fun. That went really well.

Bryn wants to ask, really? *Really?*

Is it just what people say, or does he mean it?

He says, I do these things all the time, but this one felt really natural.

Really good.

(Really?)

Bryn says, you made it easy. It was a collaboration.

And then they're at the handshake. Two hands clasped. What an odd custom. And how have they never shaken hands before? The meetings, the review, the albums that have come and gone. Never a single handshake.

Tobias' hand is warm and dry. He pulls Bryn into a hug, easily, fluidly. They embrace and then they're pulling apart again. He wants to get a beer. She does, too, but something keeps her from saying, *I'll join you.*

She'll wonder later, over and over, why she didn't say that. Not regretting it, just wondering. The words rang in the back of her mind, but they didn't sound right. Too eager, too invasive.

Not her.

She was going to stop being herself in order to lose her heart, but at the last minute she pulls up short and there she is. The self she's always been. Sure footed, heart in place.

Bryn helps Leo pack his camera, says good shoot. I think it went really well.

What she wants is to see the camera stills, to see Tobias sitting next to her. The photographic moment when he leaned in. The most extraordinary thing.

○

Door 2.

Bryn says, wait.

She doesn't want to have to be the one to say it, but what if she leaves now and never knows. All of these years of feeling things and telling herself it's just in her mind. It's just her heart feeling what it needs to feel to get in close, to see deeply, to get the story. All of these years telling herself that it's not real.

It's real, but it won't last. Just a crush. A crush on a song or an album. A crush on a made-for-stage character. A crush on what the rockstar represents. The things that she can never be but still wants to visit. Still wants to get close to.

A crush is fleeting, like a dream. It fades upon waking. It leaves no mark.

She wants to know, but she doesn't want to ask: *Did you feel it, too?*

She wants him to say it. She wants it all to be made clear.

Then again, she's felt it before. With Evan. With Jude. The prickling sense that this was more and maybe she didn't have to swallow her feelings. Smother the crush. Maybe if she gave it words, everything would be okay.

She thinks this, and immediately the voice of reason and order sets her straight.

Never try to befriend the rockstar.

This is not about you.

Never about you.

Too late. Tobias Bridge turns in the doorway. Bryn said to wait and he's waiting.

She tells herself, *this is where you take a deep breath and either say it or don't say it. Choose a way to go and commit to it.*

She says to him, that thing you did. When you leaned forward. Is that just how you do interviews?

He keeps on waiting.

Because, she says, I felt something. Like we clicked.

Tobias takes his time. Something from within is unfurling. Not that he's tight, but he lets go, unwinds, grows even lighter. Says, yeah, I thought we clicked, too.

Now Bryn waits. Breathes in and out.

Tobias says, it's what I hope will happen, you know? Because I talk about myself and my music all the time but it's just talk. It's me doing my job on one end so the person on the other end can do their job and then we both get what we want but we walk away with nothing. I don't mind that, because it's how this works. But I hope for something more.

You hope for the click, says Bryn.

Tobias leans on the door frame, tilts his hat back. He says, it's all about connection. The songs, the touring, the guitar. The singing, the festivals, the getting up on stage every night. And sometimes it works and sometimes it doesn't, but once in awhile it really, *really* works. That's what I aim for.

For people to love you back? Bryn asks.

Kind of. But I don't just want for people to love me. I mean, I do, of course I do. But then I get off stage and people slap my back and say great show and then it's done.

You want more than that.

Tobias nods. That's all good, he says, but I want to be *moved.*

For someone to fall in love with you? Bryn asks.

He says, you'd think that would be it. But sometimes that thing, when you see a girl from the stage and you know she'll ask you back to her place, and you know it'll be nice and sweet—but it's not enough. That can still end up feeling empty.

What doesn't feel empty? asks Bryn. Because she wants to know, too. She thinks that she and Tobias are two sides of a coin. He's always getting adoration, but he's holding out for the real thing. She's never getting adoration, but she's holding out for the real thing.

She's waiting to lose her heart.

At least, she's dabbling with the idea of letting her heart be lost, which, of course, is no way to lose anything.

Tobias says, it's hard to put into words what doesn't feel empty. It's like giving a name to a double negative. But I know it in the moment. The warm feeling. When you look at someone and you think, *oh, it's you. Well, I can tell you anything.*

I almost never feel that way, says Bryn.

But now you do? asks Tobias.

She nods. She wants to run away. That's enough. Enough of revealing things, admitting things, asking things. That's enough of putting herself out there. Stop now. But she doesn't stop because she's opened this metaphorical door. And because Tobias is blocking the very real door. And because she's a little bit lightheaded. She says, I kind of felt that way the first time I met you.

Before today? asks Tobias.

Yeah, says Bryn. A couple of times in the street, and once at a wine bar on New Years Eve.

We met on New Year's Eve?

Bryn nods. Says, I suggested that you order the Garnacha.

Tobias grins. He doesn't say he remembers or doesn't remember (of course he doesn't—he meets so many people, and it was years ago, and why would he?) but he smiles like he's happy that the memory exists somewhere, in someone's mind.

He says, you have anyplace you've got to be? You should come hang out with the band. Have dinner with us. We can drink that beer now, or whatever you want.

Bryn hesitates. Isn't sure if she should. Isn't sure how to be, because this isn't what she does or who she is.

But she's been thinking about being someone else. And if she were someone else, that person would stay. That person would eat dinner with the band, drink wine, chat about nothing. Maybe play video games, maybe talk set lists. Maybe just be company until the show starts.

Tobias backs into the bar. Daylight has almost completely receded from the courtyard. Bryn feels a chill in the air. Evening is falling. She has places she could go to, but no place where she has to be.

That was the question, wasn't it? *Anyplace you have to be?*

It might just be pizza, says Tobias. He's still holding the door open. The literal door.

And the metaphorical door.

To have a metaphorical door held for one is surely a sign. A sign of what, it's hard to say. Safe travels? A smooth road ahead? A cozy room? A good decision?

Bryn makes up her mind, walks toward the door, toward Tobias who doesn't say anything but who feels like an answer. And not just a yes/no answer, but a full paragraph with details and calculations. Facts and figures. Statistical data and well-turned phrases.

iii.

Door 3.

What they eat—it doesn't matter. The chatter of the band, inside jokes, easy laughter. They're together like family, and Bryn is among them. An observer, but also one of them. Her place is neither defined nor hard to understand. She sits at the table. Tobias is on her left. He passes the growler of beer to her and that wink is there again. It's a crinkle in his crows feet. A flicker of something that comes and goes, but also remains.

Bryn watches the show from the side of the stage, standing shoulder to shoulder with the road manager. She's been here before. Not right here, but close enough. With the crew, with the road manager. Learning the language of those who travel together. Coming to understand how a band is more than a lineup of musicians. It's a gypsy caravan of performers and crew, and they all have a part to play in the illusion that, together, they create each night. The thing that they breathe life into and cast out like a spell over the audience.

They talk a little bit, Bryn and Jonathan the road manager. He has stopped saying *thanks for the opportunity* and is now saying real things like, I hope Tobias' voice holds out. And, the guitar sounds good tonight. The strings were too new last night, but now they're right.

There are girls dancing in front of the stage. The Buccaneers are neither a guy band nor a chick band. They attract men and women, both. Lots of youngish couples dressed in flannel and denim. The kind of people who like music festivals and beat poetry; weekends at the beach and backpacking trips through Europe.

But the girls in front of the stage are the girls who go to shows with their hair carefully loosened and their jeans tight. They dance in a way that says, *I love this song* and also, *ask me backstage*.

Bryn feels just territorial enough to laugh at herself. She doesn't feel jealous. She doesn't expect anything—what's come out of the evening has already been more than she'd hoped for.

She'd hoped for nothing. She is as close to *being along for the ride* as she ever has been.

She does go backstage, later. She's there when the band goes back onstage for an encore. Walking up the steps, Tobias claps a sweaty hand on Bryn's shoulder. And later, after the bar clears, Bryn follows Jonathan's lead and wraps cables into figure eights. She helps box the merch, carries things to the van, ignores the impulse, each time it rises in her jittery mind, *to leave now before you've outstayed your welcome.*

Tobias says, well after midnight, come with us to the hotel. We'll be hanging out for awhile.

Bryn says, her voice pitched too high with nerves, come back to my place and hang out.

She keeps her face still, unclenches her hands, her jaw, her stomach. It's so hard to be easy in herself, which is why she's never been in a band, on the road, on a stage. Finding that sort of ease of being, or some sort of temporary escape from the self into this easier persona, has never happened for Bryn.

But Tobias is unaffected by her anxious hopefulness, her flight or fight, her sweat-prinkled palms. He says, yeah, that sounds great. Can we take your car?

○

In Bryn's apartment, Tobias is as relaxed as he is on stage. Because:

1. He never lets go of his character, this Tobias Bridge who he inhabits for the sake of his art. His work.

2. Tobias Bridge is not a character at all, but the true self of this man who inhabits the name on stage.

Bryn wonders what the name of her true self would be. She says this out loud. Who is my inner Tobias Bridge?

The musician standing near her in the kitchen says, who is my inner Bryn Thompson?

He says, I do remember you. At the bar. I remember the Garnacha. I remember thinking that you looked familiar, and that I didn't want to be the guy who said, *don't I know you from somewhere?* to the girl at the bar on New Year's Eve, when his own girlfriend was standing right behind him waiting for her glass of wine.

Bryn smirks at that. Lets herself react to the joke instead of to the relief that she feels knowing that he remembered her. Remembers her.

Will continue to hold her in his mind even when he's not in her kitchen.

She asks Tobias is there's a girlfriend now. He says for now there's just the band. That's his great romance. It won't be enough forever, but for now it's what he wants.

Sit close enough to touch, and then don't touch. Just a sliver of light between two bodies.

And then he's kissing her. A thing that if Bryn had imagined it, would have been awkward. She would have erased the thought, not allowed herself to remain in that picture. The cliché, the kitchen, the girl who asks the rockstar back to her place. The rote predictability of it.

Without precedent, though, it's the simplest of gestures. Not meant to be fought. As simple as stumbling drunk, as falling into sleep, as diving into a pool.

Tobias is not something (someone) longed for and then obtained. He's not the answer to a prayer or a wish or even a question. His kiss is not a conversation, nor is it a dance.

He, his kiss, his presence in Bryn's kitchen, the complete universe of his embrace, is something far simpler. Surfacing to blue sky through warm green water. A cherry tomato, sun-warmed and just picked, bursting on the tongue.

He pulls back says, I need a bath.

She says, you can use my tub.

Good, he says. Come with me.

○

They're together in the kitchen and in the bath. They talk and they sit in silence. They feel compelled to tell each other everything. The back story, the nuances. She makes tea, and then they open a bottle of wine.

Tobias sits naked in the tub, lazily scrubbing his limbs and then dunking his head to wash his hair. Bryn sits with him. She doesn't undress and climb in. She doesn't leave the room. She feels shy about seeing him naked, but she also feels like he's giving her something. His vulnerability. His total lack of self-consciousness.

Yes, there's a voice in her mind that says he does this all the time. The voice that tells Bryn she's acting like a groupie. That she's being the girl she always promised herself she would never be. That she's being the girl her rules are so carefully designed to keep her from being.

Never cross the barrier of touch. A handshake, yes. A quick hug. Posing side-by-side, arms around waists for a photo op, yes. But a caress? A kiss? Never.

They lie on Bryn's bed in their clothes and float. They're face to face, watching each other. Two pairs of eyes, two sets of questions. Too many options.

A. She wants to stay awake with him all night, but that is the stuff of songs and really she wants to give him the one thing he rarely gets, which is sleep. So she lifts his hat from his head and runs her fingers through his hair. Not sexy-like, but the other way. The way parents do to put children to sleep. Like her mom used to do when she was a kid. Sometimes on her back, sometimes up and down the length of her arm. The touch of sleep.

She knows she'll lose him to sleep.

B. He reaches across the sliver of space between them and touches her hip. Her back. Pulls her up against him so that their bodies pulse and beat together. His breath in her mouth. His face too close to see, just a blur of features. Damp hair, warming skin, the lingering memory of wine.

Bryn tries to think of the right questions to ask. The questions are what are important.

Why is it always love that the mind and body crave?

Why not peace, or truth, or a good mystery? Love or power, love or money, love or fame…In most cases love will ultimately lose. This isn't cynical, this is just how it goes. It's hard to sustain the flame of love. It's hard to continually stoke a thing that refuses to be defined or quantified.

Everyone says: Tell me that you love me.

Tell me why you love me.

She doesn't say any of this. She says nothing. There's nothing to ask—the questions have been absorbed by the night, by the wine, by the way the moment has stilled.

And his hand is on her back, holding her against him. Neither of them moving. There's only the rise and fall of their chests, in sync. A slow bellows fanning a slower flame.

Why you? Because it wasn't supposed to be you.

And why now?

Why here?

He says, low, so low she can barely make out the words, have we always been arriving at this moment? Or have we jumped time and fate together, and landed in this new place?

Ask the right questions.

She says, so low that he can barely make out the words, I'll jump with you.

C. If she walked through the door, at the club, if she asked Tobias Bridge why he leaned in, if she stayed for dinner and for the show and after the show. If she asked him back to her house and he came with her and they drank wine from tea cups while he soaked in her tub. If they lay, face to face on Bryn's bed, so close they could no longer tell where they began and ended. If that, then where to next?

What might have seemed like an effort in Bryn's mind, were she somewhere in the past trying to project into the future, was, in the moment, effortless.

They jumped, hand in hand. Or not hand in hand. His arm holding her against him. And it was not a jump in that they didn't plummet, but instead soared on an updraft. Hang-gliding, her body suddenly over his, both floating and pinning him to the mattress.

Because, he says, *even I forget where one of us ends and the other begins.*

Him, a butterfly, something gossamer and winged.

Her, a horse galloping, a serpent writhing, a fruit ripening.

Him, a deep reflecting pool.

The harmony of their bodies so tight not even a sheet of paper could slip between them. His hand was under her shirt, against her smooth skin and her secret scars. Against everything she kept covered and cloistered. Against what she wanted and what she didn't dare to want.

What was never spoken. What was never said.

Yes, he says.

I didn't ask anything, she says.

I want you, he says.

D. They will not return to earth. If they're in the sky, they'll remain there. Winged creatures. If they're underground, they'll stay there, eyeless and colorless, navigating the topography by feel or sonar. With their wings and with their lungs in tandem, twin bellows fanning the slow flame.

His mouth on her throat. His arms keeping her from falling away, suctioning her to him as he rolls them. They are tossed by the waves of their own amplified wanting.

They are without gravity.

They are overwhelmed by gravity. They are falling into one another.

They're fiercely hungry. Insatiable. Almost crying out from wanting and receiving, but having wanted for so long. At least one heart cracks.

Not the heart muscle, which beats on, a dauntless machine.

But the stone heart. The archaic beast in the center of the mind and its prehistoric sister at the center of the solar plexus where things hurt. Missing, longing, dreaming.

Where songs are born. And the words to describe them. Those two kinds of poetry forged at the same slow flame, the same exploded stone.

○

These are the doors. Everything begins again at this point. The hallway that they were walking down a few minutes ago, that one that was just an ordinary hallway (interview, shake hands, walk away) is now a coridor of doors. Every door is a possibility.

And man said, let us make rockstars in our image, after our likeness: and let them have dominion over things that creep upon the earth. So he created rockstars, men and women, and blessed them and said, be fruitful, and multiply, and replenish the earth. Man created rockstars in his image, fearfully and wonderfully made. Marvelous were these works.

iv.

What happens after a heart is lost? Or exercised. Or exorcised. Shaken from its slumber, the dust knocked off, the preciousness knocked off, the whole bloody, red pulp of it held up to the sun and seen clean through?

The ghosts of past loves flee to the corners of the room, because new love comes not as a champion of ghosts, but as a liberator. A lantern against the dark. A machete against the wilderness.

What happens when the rules are all broken and scattered like bottles and trash after a party so memorable no one can remember it?

What happens when everything that was known, every support beam and cross tie, every inch of tera firma, every comforting platitude, is disproven? Disqualified, disbarred. Without the structure, what remains?

Waking with Tobias Bridge (if the choice was, indeed, the third door) is hardly like waking in a burned out building. There's barely any time to begin the day together before he's gone again. And yet the morning is unhurried. Time for pancakes, time for a walk, time for a pot of coffee.

What happens next is like what happened before, only in a parallel universe where Tobias Bridge has left the imprint of his head on the pillow, where he's forgotten his neckerchief as evidence that he was there. The world still churns its treadmill.

And, surprisingly, the rules still apply. They matter less, but they work just as well. They get the job done, spinning the gears. The phone still rings. The keyboard still taps out its Morse Code messages.

Rockstars still have things to say. Tours to take, albums to release, posters to sell, stages to grace, beers to drink, autographs to sign, girls or boys waiting for something. Hard to say what. Easy to guess, hard to know for sure.

✪

Talking to Wes Grady of The Racquet is almost too comfortable. Fear is what keeps rock climbers from falling and all of that. But the way people tell you to get out of your comfort zone? Wes is an argument against that. He's somewhere between a brother and a guy who seems like a friend and then, without warning, it hits you that you're really into him.

Bryn thinks that she needs more of that in her life. More ease. More blurring of the lines between professionalism and fun.

And then she thinks that she had that. For a minute, in the arms of Tobias Bridge. She couldn't live that way, right? The late nights, the shuddering roller-coaster of adrenaline and exhaustion. The falling but not landing. Isn't this just as good? Quieter, fewer variables, less of a rush but also less of a crash. While the rest of the world is sleeping off a hangover or wriggling into pantyhose for another eight hours as a bank teller, Bryn is sipping hot coffee and talking to Wes Grady.

Thank god for the friendly guys. The ones who make it easy. The ones who are cool and laid back, but enthusiastic. Not too cool to talk, to let down their guard, to crack jokes. It's nice to just be with someone for twenty or thirty minutes, to be with the voice on the other end of the line or the smile and head of shaggy hair across the table. It's nice to not have to work at it.

There are so many cool people who work so hard at being cool, they become cold. People who measure their words and reserve their smiles. People who were voted homecoming kings and queens; people who have never been broken up with because they were always the ones who instigated the break. People who never had a zit or a cowlick or an undone fly.

You think you're an outsider, baby, that's just fine
I'm an outcast, too. You're one of my kind.
Songs are just songs. Something to dance to. Something to sing along with. They're clever rhymes that stick in the mind. But words have power, too. Mantras, hexes, invocations, incantations.

Bryn says to Wes, how will you know when you've made it? It's a question with which she's been obsessed in the past. Today, the question is less important to her, but she wants to hear what he'll say.

It's a moving target, he says. Radio play, a stadium show. Hearing my song come on the radio when I'm driving my car.

He says, I don't worry much about making it, whatever that ultimately means. We might get there. I just want to ride the wave as much as I can. Enjoy the ride.

His voice is full of the gold of autumn, the sweetness of Indian summer, glint of sun on water. He skips like a rock across the surface of a lake, smooth and unaffected.

Bryn can't help but like him.

Once, she was speaking on a panel of music writers and someone in the audience said, The people you went to high school with must be so jealous of you.

She smiled at the time, but she thought, No. No they aren't. Because

1. They never thought I was cool to begin with and

2. It's not like I'm hanging out with rockstars. They're not inviting me to their pool parties.

People from high school got excited about their classmates who became famous. They didn't get excited about their classmate who made a career out of talking to famous people. Big difference.

So there were moments when an interview with someone especially famous loomed and Bryn felt the mounting anxiety—the fear of failure juxtaposed against the pin prick of excitement.

Fame was always alluring. But niceness and ease impressed her more.

Bryn says to Wes, you took some big risks on your new record. You lead with an eight minute song. You put cello in the middle of a rocker. Was the plan to challenge the album-making process?

He says, well, we've never played it safe. We've never taken the easy way out. I want to keep it interesting, and I want to feel engaged.

He says, I have to write the songs that make me happy—the songs I want to hear and the songs I want to play.

He says, every song has to fit in the catalog. Each one has to have its place, without repeating the purpose of a previous song.

If that makes sense, he says.

✪

There are kids dancing in the pit. It might be Edward Sharpe and the Magnetic Zeros, or Mumford and Sons—one of those bands with a banjo. Played fast. Whipping the dancing kids into a frenzy. Bryn stands at the back of the room, climbing up on a chair to see better, and then climbing back down because she's already seen this.

Kids discovering a band. Kids jumping and twirling, like they've not only discovered this one band, but all music. All the music that ever has been or will be. They believe they're the first ones, the only ones.

Bryn wants to laugh, but then again, that's kind of the point, right? To feel that thing. The first-ness. The rush of first love, of the first dance, of the realization that everything good starts right now. In this very second.

It's an illusion, but it's also totally true.

Bryn climbs up on the chair again and watches the dancing kids. She feels them, lives through them vicariously. Feels called back to that part of herself who was a kid and danced in the pit and felt the world made new. Felt the breathless wonder of the lyrics, the weighty importance of it: *music is my life.*

Maybe she never was that kid. Maybe she never said those words. But even as the spectacle hits her with its silliness, its done-ness, its repetitive-ness, she's also aware of how, on some level, she gets it.

If this isn't who she is now, it's who she once was. If it wasn't who she once was, it's who she wanted to be. Meant to me. Hoped to be. And if not that, then at least the dancing kids are some sort of universal archetype.

Dirty-footed cherubs. Urban fauns and fairies. Post-modern jesters. The rag-rag progeny of Bacchus.

Or not. Maybe nothing so important.

They just look so happy.

❂

This will be our secret, the way I am with you. The way I was and maybe can't get back to being, but even if that's how it is—even if we never make it back to that low-lit and wine-tinted place—you can keep that secret in your pocket like a lucky coin or a buckeye.

This is us in the window reflection when you slipped a record from its sleeve and set it on the turntable and it was the one song that said what I would have said were I not always so busy trying to say the right thing and so worried that the wrong thing would hurt someone or reflect badly on me or burn some bridge before I ever even realized I was going to have to cross.

But never mind that, my words, my damn thoughts. There's only you, you standing there saying dance with me, and me in your arms as if I know how to be in anyone's arms.

This is how we move, when we're stripped of all the talking, when we're flesh and guts, when we're down to the nerve, when we stop the performance and let our raw seams show.

Boy, rock me now. Quick before I change my mind. Before I lose this perilous beat.

Dance me. My feet on your feet if we have to do it that way. But don't be gentle with me because my god I'm tired of this kid gloves approach to living. Break me with your softness. Wound me with your kindness, your sweet heart, your clean soul.

Make me human. Do it now, before I change my mind. A girl can't always be this strong and new. Here you are, your arms, your hips, your sway.

Make a meal of me, make a memory, bruise yourself onto me so I remember your print and then erase everything else. Consume me, incinerate me to ash, leave nothing. No trail back to who I was. Just the burn of your gaze, two perfect reflections of me. Seeing you.

Part six

i.

Bryn walked across town with her leather jacket zipped against the sting of cold air. She found her way to the club, which was really just a door into a cramped room, and sat on a barstool watching a singer and a Flamenco guitarist.

The night transformed the way nights sometimes can. By circumstance, by music, by the magic of who's met, by the alchemy of lighting. The night was transformed the way, for most people, only the rarest of nights are. And, for Bryn, the way so many nights are.

She knew this to be true and the weight of that fact hit her as hard as the brandy in her glass. Bryn slipped the napkin from under her drink and wrote on it:

This is not an ordinary life.

And then, instead of concentrating on the music, she let it color the words that ran through her mind as she jotted a letter on the napkin. A missive to some future self. Or perhaps her past self. The girl who felt less lonely in the presence of music. The girl who learned to talk to rockstars because if conversations were to be few and far between, shouldn't they be worth remembering?

This is the moment when the liquor hits, when the beat drops in a slinky pulse that thumps and rings against the blood and bones with such a sexy superhuman urgency that to deny it would be to deny life itself and whatever accident of god or science put us here.

And here we find ourselves, outside of the ordinary, tucked into a cupboard of recycled air and crumpled dreams. We duck in to escape the cold and to take solace in a moment or two—perhaps an hour—of fantasy and warm-lit betterment. The stoking of our imaginations which are not, in fact, make-believe, but the embers of our best selves and brightest hopes that we allow to live and burn.

Here we gather like winos around a trash can fire, warming our chapped fingers and combining our scraps of drink into one jewel-toned bottle which we pass from lip to lip and kindle our embers.

We do not look into each other's eyes but remain strangers in shared space.

Then again, we're not strangers. We're all called to this place, to this dream, to this song, to this vision of our highest selves. And we don't even need to speak the names of our best versions because in the plush grip of liquor and candlelight and music that is what is known.

And that is why we're here. And that is why we lay our moments like offerings at the altar of the extraordinary life. And that is why, when we return to the cold beyond this room, we no longer feel its bite or chill. For a while the glow carries us as much as we carry it. And that's enough.

When she was done, Bryn folded the napkin into her pocket and left a dollar beside her empty glass. She zipped her coat again against the cold and stepped into the night.

The city had been transformed by a thin layer of new white snow. The air sparkled with it and in the reach of a street light, tiny ice crystals glittered and danced. The hush seemed to swell all around and somewhere far above the cityscape, surely stars shone. Surely.

Looking out the window at blowing snow, the day as grey as old towels, Bryn let her mind drift while a song played through her headset.

Her boss tapped on the doorframe, making her jump. His mouth moved.

What?

I said your ears have gotten bigger.

She laughed a fake, tinny laugh and dropped the headset back over her ears. A week had passed since she'd been offered an editorship and she hadn't replied. It would mean more money, more job security, more responsibility in shaping the voice of the magazine. But it would also mean less of her own writing.

Fewer conversations with musicians.

Just the thought gave Bryn a hollow feeling in her chest. But then again, wasn't change good? Wasn't life about moving on, evolving?

But maybe this idea of motion—moving toward something, moving away from something—was just an illusion. Bryn had a friend in college who was a religious studies major until she discovered Buddhism in her sophomore year. By the time the friend was a junior, she'd dropped out of school and moved into a retreat center in Connecticut.

I've spent a month in silent meditation in my room, she wrote to Bryn once. *I thought I'd miss travel and adventure and everything that happens in the outside world. But I don't miss anything. I've learned that the world is all right here, and I only have to sit and wait for it to come to me.*

Bryn's initial reaction was to be horrified. At the time she was at the height of her infatuation with Preston Schotte. She only wanted to be more out, more involved, more engaged, more implicated, more experienced, more a part of the world. Bryn couldn't imagine pulling back from all of that, putting on the brakes to sit in a room for a month. Not even for a day. Not even for an hour—not without someone interesting there with her.

Now, most of twenty years later, Bryn still doesn't get it. But the words come back: *I've learned that the world is all right here, and I only have to sit and wait for it to come to me.*

Writing is sort of like that. Letting the world reveal itself. Or, more to the point, forming the world. Writing it into being.

✪

Can you miss people who you've never even known? Is it possible to feel them moving, breathing, waking from some opposite corner of the world? Are people somehow bound by shared molecules, crossed DNA and linked desires? Or are we all separate entities moving like robotic mice on tireless treadmills?

Why do the leaves change from the top of the tree down?

Bryn presses her fingertips against her eyes. She files the review she was working on. Words torn from her psyche and given their own life in the world. Words that will either set out in search of adventure and fortune, finding their way into a press kit or album notes or a blog post somewhere, or else stagnate and fall flat, never leaving the one-dimensional plane of the page.

But what of all the musicians who she's thought of, dreamed of, invested her time in? Do they feel her as she feels them? It's a question that, when she's tired and dusk is falling, can haunt her.

Most days, when the existential angst finds her, Bryn turns her back on it. She plays dance music, walks briskly, goes out for dinner, buys a bottle of wine. TV helps, so does the radio. Sitting in a noisy coffee shop trying to eavesdrop on other people's conversations helps. Existential angst can be put off indefinitely. It keeps knocking but there's no real reason to let it in.

Why? It's existential because it's unanswerable. *Why are we here? Is there a god? Are we connected to other people or are we alone?*

There are no answers because, even if there were, it wouldn't matter. We are here, and knowing our purpose changes neither our here-ness nor the fact that someday we will cease to be.

If there is a god, that god does not need our belief to exist.

Even if we are alone, isn't it better to hope for connection? And, perhaps, in hoping, we create connection.

Desire is a powerful force.

Bryn stops pressing her eyes, waits for the flurry of black dots to clear from her vision field and then checks her email.

There's one from Andrea.

Jude is in town. Your town. Checking out art galleries for a spring exhibition. You should call him.

Bryn thinks, *No.* The ghost of him has finally left. The need, the hope for something. What? His attention? His recognition? His warm eyes resting on her face?

A brush of his fingertips. A song, a word. Her name spoken in his voice. An hour, a walk, a stretch of silence shared in the frosty air. Time to know if this thing is a thing or just a false emotion gleaned from too many hours spent alone with an album and a database of photos.

A crush. A silly crush that crushes at pride and dignity and the tender part of the heart that wants to love for the sake of loving the way an acrobat wants to somersault through the air for the love of cheating gravity.

Bryn thinks no, but her hands type yes. *Yes. Tell me his number. I'll call him.*

Do that, says Andrea. *He likes you.*

Likes me? No. He doesn't even remember me. He doesn't answer my emails.

Hush. Don't leave my boy to wander around all by himself.

No, says Bryn. *I wouldn't do that.*

Of course you wouldn't, says Andrea. *That's why I got in touch.*

○

She looks at her hair in the mirror of the office bathroom. It's not a nice bathroom. It's clean but gloomy and the mirror casts Bryn's image back, flat and pale. She pinches at her cheeks the way junior high girls do to look like they're wearing blush. The girl version of doing a dozen pushups. It's hopeless, she's still just herself in a black blazer and striped t-shirt, flyaways escaping from her ponytail. Nothing glamorous.

In the movie version of her life, Bryn thinks she'd have a fragile Julie Delphy prettiness with rosy cheeks and pink lips. She'd look at home in a satin dress, ethereal instead of bedraggled.

In the movie version of her life, the mirror in the office bathroom would be lit by a soft yellow bulb and when she gazed at herself a waltzy song by Pepper Rabbit would play. Then she'd zip up her jacket and pull on fingerless gloves that look cool without causing her fingers to freeze. She'd take her phone from her pocket and, leaning casually against a lamp post, she'd dial his number.

And he'd answer, breathless, glad to hear from her.

So what if this is not a movie? And so what if she's shaking, all nervous rattle and chattering teeth? The past love (which was never really love but something that is easier just to call love and file away as silly) comes back in an embarrassing flush of woozy excitement and dread.

Love is just a word for things that are felt intensely but which defy logic. *Real* love is faded and threadbare, soft around the edges, predictable and reassuring. The feel and smell of slept-in flannel sheets. Pancake breakfasts. A cool cloth on a feverish forehead. Something that can grow old, dog-eared, familiar.

The other thing, the electric glance, the air-sucked-out-of-a-room vertigo, the speed-and-butterflies knocking in the chest: That's just chemistry. Hormones, pheromones, right-place-at-right-time-ness.

There's no magic to love at first sight. Make peace with that and keep going.

Bryn smoothes her hair and straightens her jacket, leaves the bathroom and goes back to her desk where she surveys the darkening world. Dusk is hard, but night is fine. Darkness hides the flaws of day and allows a certain limitlessness. Possibility.

Bryn takes out her phone and dials Jude Archer. And, on the other end of the line, it rings. And she waits.

✪

She'll think back later and remember it this way: The streets are strangely empty. Daylight has given way to early darkness and the raw chill that marks any number of generic winter days. Days for which there is no reason to recall. And yet every detail will come back to her, even though, as it's happening, she doesn't remind herself to notice. The click of her heels against the sidewalk, the few black-coated shoppers bustling in and out of stores. Everyone has a place to be and they're only in the street as a quick aside to the main events of their evenings.

But Bryn feels suspended in the outside world. The walk to the gallery takes forever. Her own footfall is monotony and still she could go on forever, a step at a time, in no rush to arrive.

Bryn has never been in a hurry to meet her destiny. Words have given her minutes and hours, lingering in a time that's come and gone. A single song, a piece of music, a quote, a particular turn of phrase. These she revisits and reconsiders, mulling them and turning them in her mind, letting her adjectives fall and regroup, reconfigure until they find their own way. A moment passes, but the retelling of it goes on and on, allowing it to live on.

By writing down the moments, Bryn has preserved what could have been dew evaporating in sunlight. She's given weight to the fleeting and polish to the mundane. She has chosen, with her own words, which moments to let slip away and which to keep.

This moment, though, walking to the gallery, down a familiar street, is not one she chooses to hold on to. This is just a walk. It's just a favor to Andrea. It's just the route to get to the gallery where a musician she once met just happens to be. Alone and perhaps in need of company.

It's nothing.

Bryn turns a corner, strides through sounds of people moving away from the moment and into other lives, other times. They leave the inbetween-ness which she inhabits. The air is scented with Chinese food and then with laundry soap. Lives flash and blow out like candles, but in their wake they leave traces. Litter, wrappings, shells, things forgotten, crumpled papers, receipts, accolades, footprints, petals, crumbs, perfume lingering, a resonant hum, sparks against the void.

The window of the gallery is steamy. A warm room floating like a bubble above the cold evening. Bryn tells herself that months have passed now and the click and rush, the psychic need—all of it has faded now. She may not even recognize Jude Archer.

But then he's there, his back to her as he studies a large canvas. The room swirls around him. A bell on the door rings.

See me now.

She'll remember later that she feels the heat of the gallery hit her face. The lights are warm, there's some sort of music playing softly. Jazz.

Jude Archer turns from the canvas as if he's been expecting her. His face is open. He crosses the room to meet her.

His eyes are wide-set, brown and flecked with gold. There's so much light behind them. He's lit from within. A candle. A torch against an opulent sky.

She remembers it like this, though there is no sky. Just the white-washed ceiling and recessed lighting. Just the backdrop of abstract art, of a few milling onlookers, the expectant gallery owner and his black-clad assistants.

See me now.

He wraps her in a hug, his wool coat scratchy against her face. He smells like snow and sleep, of incense smoke and faintly of acrylic paint. She buries her face in his chest, until he steps back, his hands gripping her shoulders.

Bryn, says Jude Archer.

Don't leave my boy to wander around all by himself, said Andrea. So Bryn stays by his side. She asks, do you have your work here? She says, tell me about what you're painting these days.

He leads her to a leather couch and they sink into it, side by side. He shows her on his iPad. Everything is red, white and black. The faces of women pout with plump red lips and bat huge eyes ribbed with tarantula lashes.

Is there a story line? Bryn asks.

He says he just paints, lets his mind go empty and loses himself in the gesture.

Do they speak to you, later? After you paint them?

He leans toward her, his long leg brushing hers. Sometimes, he says.

Is there a connection between your paintings and songs?

I don't think so. Sort of, but not in any obvious way. They're both what come through when I open myself up to…

The universe? she asks.

Possibly, he says.

They put on coats and walk into the deepening evening in search of dinner.

○

There's something about sharing a meal for the first time. Even grilled cheese sandwiches and fries. Ordering in front of someone, taking bites, navigating the chewing and the talking. It's the most mundane of activities and yet it's almost more intimate than sex.

So, of course, you work on acting normal. You make small talk. You would order a beer to lessen the gathering storm of nerves. You would do that, only the person across the table doesn't drink any more and so ordering a beer for yourself seems wrong.

But somewhere in the quiet attic of your mind you think, *if I could just get drunk, and get him drunk, this would be a breeze. Start with the Formica and vinyl of the fluorescent-lit booth, move to the streets, to a the relative anonymity of a club somewhere, exchange boozy, boubon-flavored kisses against a doorway in the cold before landing in a tangle of sheets and limbs.*

But then what? Then you wake to face yourself and a naked stranger. You know nothing. You want to feel love, or something like love, but what you feel is disdain. And hung over.

He says, what are you thinking, quiet girl?

Ah. Nothing. Sorry, just got lost in my mind for a moment.

Truth or dare.

She says, I'm not playing truth or dare with you.

Why?

I'm not fourteen. I know better now.

He says, too bad. He leans back.

Fine. I was wondering if you miss your days of getting wasted. I mean, I know you're happier and healthier and it seems like you're more productive now. I was just wondering—

What it would be like to go down the rabbit hole together?

She feels herself flush, the heat rising from her collar. She looks at her hands, looks at the window, flips the menu over.

He says, what I learned is that the rabbit hole remains. And maybe we'll get there. But I like being here, too.

You do?

He laughs.

They eat sandwiches and watch the people passing outside. The diner feels like an island adrift in a city of night and cold, a refuge from strangers and responsibilities. Bright lights, greasy heat, a case of whipped cream-topped pies. Jude insists they order a slice and share it. And when the oversized slice of pie arrives, with mugs of coffee, he moans that he'll get fat.

Don't be ridiculous, says Bryn.

He flicks a forkful of whipped cream at her, hitting her cheek.

He stops being a rockstar and turns into a tall guy with too many tattoos and a sharp aim with pie filling.

Bryn dips her coffee spoon into the pie and flicks it back at him, splattering his nose and chin. He grins, leaving it there, sipping coffee while holding her eyes with his.

She stops being a journalist and turns into a girl with a ponytail and decent vocabulary. She lets down her guard, laughs at his dumb jokes.

186

When the check comes she takes it, says, I'll pay. Everyone knows there's no money in the music business.

He nods in agreement, digs out a few dollars for a tip. So, what's next? he asks.

Do you need to be somewhere?

Not until noon tomorrow.

She says, then we could go to a movie, or check out a band, or walk off that pie.

Walk it is, says Jude Archer, pushing the door open for her.

But the outside world has changed. With him it's not isolated or dark. It shines. Everything holds mystery and seems to gleam with possibility. Everything that Bryn knows backwards and blindfolded shows a new face. Streets hold stories.

I love this city, says Jude.

Bryn threads her arm through his, falls into sync with his stride. She says, then give me the tour. I want to see it through your eyes.

The trust me tour?

What's that?

He says, that's when I lead the way, and you trust me.

She says, okay.

Just like that? No woman ever just says *okay*.

So I guess you better make the most of this rare occasion.

You're right, he says. And quick, before you change your mind.

But she won't change her mind. She made it up months earlier. She's already been walking down this road.

○

Sometimes two people can slip through the chain link fence of time and escape. Sometimes they make this escape by accident, unaware that they're leaving the path, or that there was even a path to leave.

Sometimes two people can steal away, into the dark or an unused room, and there in the quiet and empty space they can find some healing. Maybe they didn't even know that they needed to be healed. The chronic ache of loneliness, the scars of addiction, the clenched jaw of stress, shoulders tight from curling the body inward to protect the solar plexus. They just felt normal. Fine. Everything was fine. And then, suddenly, alone in a corner of a park or the shade of a tree, alone in an empty office or a darkened

187

theater, they find themselves in possession of some magic touch or word. A spell, an amulet, a key.

Maybe they know themselves, then, to be healers. Or maybe the healing just comes from being. From passing through each other's space, from sharing the right combination of words, from trading the right number of molecules. Maybe it's only later, after they've parted, that they realize what was broken is now whole. What hurt no longer hurts.

Sometimes the healing is just the lightest touch. A whisper, a breeze barely glancing the surface.

More often it's a heavy thing, the heat of breath and weight of bodies. Grace and the letting go of grace, because we're the prisoners of gravity and can't float around each other the way we might if we lived in the sea or the air. Instead, our land bodies knock and press against each other, the inside arm is always dead weight trapped between two torsos.

It's a clumsy dance and still we return to it. Why?

Secretly, do we hope to be healed?

Or is it only biology, the chemical calling of blood and sweat driving us to collide? What do we hope for? What is the best that could come of a momentary sharing of fingers and mouths, bodies fit in awkward configurations, a myth of oneness?

Sometimes two people enter into this tangle of limbs and come through the burning confusion unscathed.

She leans toward him under the stairs. It's a birthday party. They're both fifteen. They've come here separately to hide from the others, to regain equilibrium in this close space. They find each other and neither is surprised.

So then what? They are a pair of pale blond twins. When their lips touch, everything changes. Just a subtle shift, but still. Those few moments together undo the many days and weeks of being alone.

And they crawl back out from the basement staircase and return to the party, strangers again.

The lucky are those who come to know when they've been healed. When the hairline fractures of psyche and soul are mended by the unexpected touch of a stranger.

iv.

Something about the human condition makes it hard to recall pain. Joy remains but pain eventually recedes into the mist. Sure, joy loses its sharpness. Its colors dull and blur but there's something about the soft proportions that it takes on over the years. Soft as a worn bandana, as lived-in denim, as flannel sheets.

Neither do memories retain their sharpness with years or experience or the accumulation of those mental Polaroids. Instead, with practice, you seem to get better at washing them in pastel light and soft focus until everything in the past takes on a twilit, cotton-candy glow.

Each day begins as a blank canvas of sorts. A new world, unexplored, and in the vacuous newness you do what you've always done. Get up. Turn on the coffee maker. Maybe take a jog or watch the morning shows. Maybe burn the toast or roll over for another ten or twenty minutes of sleep. Routines anchor the unknown and bridge the expanse of limitless possibility.

Dress. Put on mascara. Brush teeth. Pack a bag, find the keys, lock the door behind.

And then at the end of the day, reverse the process: Unlock the door, put away the keys, unpack the bag. Brush teeth, remove mascara, undress and slide back into bed.

The bookends of routine: As if what happens between wake and sleep can be measured out and controlled. So many pairs of headlights. So many rain-spattered windows. So many cracks in the sidewalk.

Some sidewalk cracks are only flaws in the concrete. Others are impromptu gardens for dandelions.

There are secret places in the city that open up like hidden worlds. Gates left ajar just enough to serve as an invitation to darkened narrow walkways that open into lush jungles of vines and shade. Closet-sized pockets of the primeval that exist outside of routine, outside of order. Reminders that beyond well-timed meals, folded towels, dental floss, bill payments, birthday cards, evening news, alarm clocks, weight repetitions, vitamins, laundry loads and transit tickets, wilderness lurks.

And, eventually, it will win. Eventually it will send its dandelions up through all the cracks. It will choke the power poles and the glass facades, it will creep and flourish in the unwatched spaces. It will bloom and pulse and fall and rot and begin again, no matter the tick of the ordinary.

The wilderness will claim all the memories, all the pains and joys, all the failures and triumphs. It will consume what has been and what is yet to be, coming with the force of a tidal wave. Buds burst and grow into leaves and then fall away. Trees change color from the top down; but metamorphosis is from the ground up. A dark force of oblivion.

And still. You catch sight of the gate. A gate that must have always been there, on your walk home. A walk you've taken hundreds of times down this same block. And suddenly you see it, and it calls to you, and you go in. You leave your path and enter this unknown universe, which will destroy the you who you have always been, but you're not afraid.

You think it smells so earthy, so green. So familiar and yet so exotic. You think you could curl up here and dream the dreams you've meant to dream for so many nights but can't quite call to your subconscious mind.

You think it smells of flowers and of the dust of comets.

✪

Jude Archer has been here before, but not sober. Not in this lifetime. He says, *in some ways we carry with us the children we once were. In other ways, we're born new each morning. To sleep is to die, to wake is to be reborn. We wake in the frequencies of who we were when we left in the night, but we're not the same. We're living with hand-me-down memories, desires and coordinates.*

She says, *if that's so, then what are dreams? How can we remember dreams if we're not dreaming but dying?*

He thinks about this. The garden is all indecipherable shapes. Bare branches press skyward. Something brushes Bryn's cheek. Fingers of pine, aromatic and feathery.

Maybe we dream our deaths, Jude says. His breath casts ghostly clouds into the space between them.

Then we should stay awake all night so that in the morning we'll still be the same two people, Bryn says.

✪

Perhaps the night is not a world apart from the world you inhabit, but a bridge across the morass. And usually you sail smoothly from one black shore to the other in a boat of sleep, but if you stay awake for the journey you can see the architecture of this link. You can kick the scaffolding, if you choose, or walk out on the platform over echoing emptiness. You can shout your own name into the chasm below, and it won't bounce back to you. It will fall forever.

But you won't fall. You'll walk, one step at a time, across miles of trestle. You listen for a train in the distance, squint your eyes in hopes of making out a horizon. There's nothing. It's like when you were small and you spent the night in the stone house of your baby sitter. She tucked you in under the heft of a feather tick and you drifted off. When you woke in the night, confused in a strange bed, you opened your eyes but the darkness was so complete, your dreams continued in the air in front of you like your own private film screening.

In the absence of light there is nothing, and everything that once was ceases to be, and you, too, will be swallowed by the fathomlessness of it all.

Not true, he says. *You're alive in sound, in smell, in taste. You can wake up to each of these senses.* His hand is in your hand and the bridge is firmly beneath your feet.

You're here now. You've always been here.

And so the two of you walk on, into the unknown. Which is, in fact, the known. After the darkness comes the dawn. You walk, arm in arm, out of the hidden garden, off the bridge, past the neighborhood at the edge of the universe and back to the streets and buildings you know. Doorways you've entered before. Diners where you've ordered breakfast, cafes where you've sat behind steamy windows drinking cups of coffee and plotting the day.

You walk through the night and enter the next day, which arrives in shades of gray and lavender, a sky streaked with a watercolor kit of pastels. The clouds that loomed ominous just hours before are suddenly cotton candy pink and peach. The sky cradles the city in its dome lid. There's no place to go but here.

You agree without saying a word to return to the place where you began. A red vinyl booth in a non-descript restaurant. The menu has changed from dinner to breakfast. One of you asks for pancakes and the other for an omelet. Toast, jam, a pot of coffee. You sit in silence over warm mugs, letting the molecules return and settle. You steal glances at each other and stifle giggles at a joke that goes unsaid.

In the beginning, you were a child, lost in the world. You learned to follow sounds, letting music guide you. You were a small boat, tossed on a wild sea. Sometimes you held on for dear life, white knuckled on the rapids and storm swells. Sometimes you drifted easily, lulled to sleep.

Adrift, you made friends with the stars and chanted their names like a mantra against loneliness. Sirius, Arcturus, Betelgeuse, Rigel.

The Rolling Stones, Van Morrison, Astrud Gilberto, Solomon Burke, Annie Lennox, The Red Hot Chili Peppers, Sade, Fishbone, The Temptations. Mazzy Starr, The Flying Burrito Brothers, Tina Turner, Nat King Cole.

You found, after a time, that the stars sometimes said your name back to you. You found that, as much as they sang to you, they spoke, too, and sometimes you were the only one who could hear.

And so you began to transcribe their stories.

Make us sound smart, they said. Make us sound cool. Cooler than we really are.

So you did. You wrote their words on sheets of paper and those sheets lay out across the expanse of the sea like stepping stones. You dared yourself to walk out on that paper bridge, one foot in front of the other, and before you knew it the shore was in sight.

Then you were no longer a child, and you were no longer lost.

V.

Stories don't really end. They just come to a punctuation mark and rest for awhile. They can't end, because endings are permanent and stories are malleable. Time, circumstance, the fading of memory—all of these blur the edges and rewrite the plot.

So there are countless possibilities for the story of Bryn and Jude. Here are a few:

✿

One
The moon is barely a sliver pinned against the night. But even in its waxing phase it's backlit, its full, round body visible to the naked eye. It's a moon of new things, of potential.

Inside, out of sight of the moon and its prevue, there are couples in bars basking in candlelit glow, searching each other's faces for starts of poems.

We're not living in a time of poetry, says Bryn.

Jude says, but there was slam. Not all that long ago.

There still is slam. It's just not relevant any more.

There's still hip-hop, says Jude.

It's just skirting the issue, says Bryn. No one has the time for novels or the patience for poetry.

She's holding the phone against her ear. His breath hangs in the spaces between words. The questions matter, but so does the silence.
- *When you listen to music, do you hear the instrumental or the vocals?*
- *Do you write the music first or the words? Does one support the other, or are they two parts of the same thing?*

(They're two parts of the song, he would say.

Yes, of course, but if we weren't talking about a song…

He says, but we are, aren't we?

Yes. Maybe. But not only songs. We're speaking of art and of creating.)

• *If I asked you to recite a poem for me now, by memory, what poem would you recite?*

• *Have you ever made one of those things, those word clouds, that show which words you use the most?*

(He says, no, but I could tell you yours: Darkness, blue, stars, night, music, dreams, echo, silence.

I like those words, she says.

He goes on. Bridge, trajectory, light, buoyant, emotive, shimmer, glitter, fathomless: This is the magnetic refrigerator poetry of your soul.)

• *Is there such a thing as a song with no music?*

• *Where does inspiration come from?*

• *Is the devil in the details, or is god?*

Closeness matters, but so does distance. Sometimes you can only really see New York from Los Angeles or Paris, or from the height of an airplane as it banks, coming back around above the city before pointing earth-wise. From that place, high above everything, worries are minimized, noise is muffled, the smell of rot and exhaust is gone, as are the decaying buildings and chain link fenced parks. From that height it's all just twinkling lights and possibility.

(*Possibility*, he says. *That one, too.*)

Sometimes you can hear a song better with your eyes closed.

○

Two

The blond girl kisses the dark-haired boy. He's either tired or drunk. She's walking away, his eyes are closing.

You've got to be Jack Kerouac, says the guy on the next bar stool. He's short, his hair has been cut just hours earlier. He's hiding his age behind expensive clothing. He's a club promoter. He washes his dinner down with a Spanish Cabernet.

A clinking sound rises and falls away. It could be laughter or ice cubes. It could be a mirage.

• *What if there were no new sounds. Is this possible? Have all the sounds already been made?*

• *Is music affected by the sounds around us? For example, could there have been industrial music prior to the industrial revolution?*

• *If you could create a new sound, what would it be like?*

Bryn still likes to tell the story of how she met Tobias Bridge for the second time. It was in a tapas bar. She suggested the Garnacha and he ordered it. (She tells it now, in the light of knowing so much more of him, but even so, she can tap that clarity of not yet knowing.)

She loves the story because it's such a *nothing* anecdote. It could have happened to anyone. All those years of interviewing rockstars, of asking such carefully-prepared questions.

And then, there he was. In his velvet jacket and shined shoes, looking at the menu.

She didn't say, I love your music (though she does) or, your last album was your most fully-realized (though it was, and she saved those songs in a special playlist for the songs that tell her something about *herself*) or, how do you maintain your energy for the duration of a show?

Instead: Go for the Garnacha. It's good.

And he said, okay.

It felt like so little, but it was the beginning of so much.

○

Three

Evan Lassiter has cut off his hair. This is a milestone, though Bryn is doing her best to act normal. It won't do to blurt, you cut your hair! Because:

1. That would be completely amateur and

2. He probably already knows.

So, what's new? she asks.

It hasn't been that long since their last interview. That was autumn, this is early spring. So early that it could just be a trick, but there's a quality to the sunlight and the scent of wet earth warming. Blood stirring. Sap rising.

He gestures toward his head. This, I guess.

Yes. Pretty big change.

I haven't had short hair since I was, like, twelve, he says.

So why now?

He shrugs. Just woke up one morning and thought, why not? Why not see who's hidden under all that hair.

And?

Another shrug. Says, it's a process. Evan's eyes are more clear, more alarmingly blue than ever.

You think this will affect your songwriting?

He looks at her for a minute, as if he's considering this for the first time. He says, Bryn, I never wrote songs with my *hair*.

She laughs at this, thinks, *I love you. You don't need to know that. But you're in my heart.*

He says, you look good, Bryn.

○

Four

Jude Archer's art exhibit opens. The gallery is scented with frangipani blooms, which must have been no small feat to find in this part of the world. The delicate blossoms float in glass bowls transferring their airy, clean perfume to the room.

Everything feels heady and weightless. Jude, full of surprises, has traded his usual black and white palette for pastel shades. His figures, formerly skeletal and tortured, are gauzy and angelic, drifting upward on the canvases. Bryn finds herself sucking in her breath.

Change is afoot. Or, perhaps, change is always in progress. The real story would be if nothing changed. That Jude found new colors is really nothing new. That Bryn might embark on a new job—maybe as a publicist, maybe as a tour manager, maybe as a novelist—that was always in the plan.

Why was the story always about what was different? Because change marks the road.

The road to where?

To anywhere.

She says to him, some other time, when they're away from the narcotic dream of winged beings and frangipani perfume, *these are the rules.*

Okay, he says.

- Rule number 1: Listen more than you speak. Remember that this isn't about you, that your job is to extract answers, not dazzle with your knowledge and cool.
- Rule number 2: Do your research and ask good questions. And distill those questions to their essence for maximum impact and minimal wordiness (see Rule 1).

- Rule number 3: Built rapport, but don't try to win the rockstar as a friend. This is not about you, this is about your readers and their relationship with the rockstar. You are not on a date. You're not going to hang out. You're not going to become pen pals. No one is going to dedicate an album to you. Or remember your name five minutes after you hang up the phone.
- Rule number 4: There are no exceptions to Rule 3.

He says, Those are good rules, but of course they only get you so far.
What do you mean? She smoothes her hair behind her ears.
Well, there are exceptions to *every* rule.

○

She says to him, some other time, maybe during a late night phone call, or maybe in one of the millions of conversations she carries on with him in the non-stop terminal of her own imagination,
Tell me about the truck stops in France.
Really? What made you think of that?
I've wondered for a long time, says Bryn. But it wasn't right for the story.
And now?
She says to him, maybe through email, or maybe on an all-night walk through the secrets of the darkened city, or maybe on a trans-Atlantic flight to a place she's pictured many times and longs to see with her own eyes—she says, this is a different story. We tell this one however we want to.
And then he doesn't say anything at all, because silence is its own sort of conversation.

Acknowledgements

I owe a great deal of gratitude to Joe, Sean and Tyler who unknowingly inspired important aspects of this story. Your songs provide a soundtrack to my life: thank you. And to all the musicians working so hard—often for so little compensation—to keep us all dancing and dreaming: you are my heroes. Thank you to my early readers, Aiyanna, Taiyo and Toni: your insights and ideas were hugely helpful. Thanks to Jason, Michael, Carla and Angela for your support, encouragement and understanding of the music-literature connection. And to Steve and Krys of Logosophia: thank you for believing in *How to Talk to Rockstars*. You are the rockstars of the small press world.

Alli Marshall grew up in Western New York and has called the mountains of North Carolina home for more than 20 years. She completed her MFA in creative writing at Goddard College and has been an arts writer and editor at *Mountain Xpress*, Asheville's alternative newsweekly, since 2003. *How to Talk to Rockstars* is her first novel. Her website is http://alli-marshall.com